MONTANA SUNRISE

MONTANA SUNRISE

•

CHARLENE BOWEN

AVALON BOOKS
THOMAS BOUREGY AND COMPANY, INC.
401 LAFAYETTE STREET
NEW YORK, NEW YORK 10003

© Copyright 1997 by Charlene Bowen
Library of Congress Catalog Card Number: 96-95279
ISBN 0-8034-9189-1

PRINTED IN THE UNITED STATES OF AMERICA
ON ACID-FREE PAPER
BY HADDON CRAFTSMEN, SCRANTON, PENNSYLVANIA

To Sue, with love

Chapter One

Shannon felt a stab of panic as she recognized Clint Gallagher's tall figure ambling down the sidewalk toward her.

Even though he was still almost half a block away, there was no mistaking the self-assured grace with which he moved, or those long, purposeful strides. Hadn't she spent much of her childhood and teen years gazing after him in rapt adoration? Hadn't she taken note of his every move, until his walk, his manner of speaking, everything about him was as familiar to her as her own reflection in the mirror?

He'd changed in the ten years since she'd seen him, of course. Fresh out of college then, although he was already taller than average, he hadn't started to fill out yet and still had the wiry, whipcord-lean build of the very young. Now, even from this distance, she could see that his shoulders had broadened, although his waist and hips were still as trim as ever. He'd been little more than a boy the last time she saw him, but there was no doubt that the figure coming toward her was that of a *man.*

And the thought of meeting him face-to-face scared her half to death!

Fortunately, Clint hadn't noticed her yet, but any second he would glance up and a flash of recognition would cross his features. She wasn't ready for that. Oh, she knew she was going to have to face him sometime. Now that she had returned to the small Montana town that was home to her, she couldn't expect to go on avoiding him indefinitely—after all, he did live on the neighboring ranch, so their paths were sure to cross. She didn't want that first meeting to be on Liberty's main street, though, where half the town might be watching. Besides, she needed time to prepare herself, to perfect the cool, impersonal smile that would convey to him that she had taken to heart his long-ago assertion that there could never be anything between them except friendship.

He was coming closer. Shannon looked wildly up and down the street, which was lined with stores and businesses, then ducked into the nearest doorway. Once inside, she took up a position off to one side of the window, where she could look out without being seen.

And right in the nick of time, she thought. Clint was just approaching. From her vantage point she was able to study him as he passed by. The only thing that didn't appear to have changed was his crisp dark hair—at least, what was visible of it beneath the wide-brimmed Stetson he wore. It looked as thick and wavy as ever. And her fingers still ached to reach up and touch it.

His craggy face, bronzed by years of working outdoors in the wind and sun, was set into stern lines. From this angle she couldn't see his dark eyes, which had once twinkled with laughter. Judging from the set of his jaw and his firm, uncompromising mouth, though, she sensed that if she were to look into those eyes now she would find them as flat and unreadable as stone.

He looked so *serious.* He used to be outgoing and fun-loving, but now his expression had a distant, remote quality, as if he had erected a wall to shut everyone out. She recalled her mother writing that he seemed "bitter." Well, that was understandable, she thought, after all that had happened.

She'd been so intent on her scrutiny that it wasn't until Clint was out of sight that she noticed chuckles coming from behind her. She became aware of a beery, stale cigarette odor. As she turned around she realized the place where she had hastily taken refuge was a small tavern, known simply as Curly's. It was named after the proprietor, a large man whose head was as devoid of hair as the proverbial billiard ball. Peering into the smoky gloom, she saw that several customers, apparent regulars, were sitting at the bar, watching her with amused grins.

"Come in for a quick snort?" one grizzled old cowboy asked.

"Have a seat, li'l lady," another patron, who had obviously spent the better part of the afternoon partaking of Curly's stock, invited. He patted the stool beside him. "Lemme buy you a drink."

Even Curly, drying glasses behind the bar, looked at her quizzically. His clientele didn't usually include attractive young women.

Although Shannon felt her cheeks flaming, she was determined to hide her embarrassment from the men at the bar. Tossing her head lightly, in a gesture that set her rich auburn hair swinging in lustrous waves, she forced herself to face them all squarely. "I just came in to—to look for someone," she asserted. The glint in her gold-flecked green eyes almost dared any of them to question her.

She scanned the faces of the men, then said, "No, I don't see him here." With as much aplomb as she could muster, she turned and walked out.

Once she was back out on the street her sense of humor took over as she realized the impression she must have made by bursting into the tavern as if she were being pursued. She smiled to herself. At least she'd provided a slight diversion for Curly's customers.

Looking down the street, Shannon couldn't suppress a ripple of excitement as she watched Clint's retreating form. Even after all this time, just the sight of him had the power to set her pulse racing. On her sixteenth birthday he'd told her, as gently as possible, that what she felt for him was merely infatuation, that she was too young to know her own mind. Someday, he'd said, she'd find someone else who would make her forget all about him.

He'd been wrong. Even at sixteen she'd known, as surely as if it had been decreed by the gods before the beginning of time, that Clint was the only man she would ever love.

But any hope she'd had that he might, in time, come to see her as something more than just "the kid next door" had been effectively dashed shortly after that when he'd announced his engagement to a girl he'd met at college.

Fortunately for Shannon, or maybe *un*fortunately—

she wasn't sure whether it was easier to see him married to someone else, or not to see him at all—Clint and his bride Valerie had taken up residence in Los Angeles shortly after the wedding.

There had been a good deal of head-shaking among the citizens of Liberty over the move. The general consensus was that it was the old "how ya gonna keep 'em down on the ranch?" syndrome, that having been away to college and seen other places, he was no longer content to spend the rest of his life in a remote section of Montana.

Those who were close to the family knew that wasn't the case, of course. She recalled an overheard conversation between her mother and Clint's. "It seems they have some kind of 'agreement,' " Evelyn Gallagher had said, shaking her head. Apparently they planned to move back to the ranch in a few years, but Valerie, accustomed to southern California's sprawling cities and sunny beaches, wanted to ease into ranch life gradually. In the meantime, Clint would put the managerial skills he'd learned in college to use working for Valerie's uncle, who manufactured air conditioners.

Air conditioners, Shannon had thought with a shudder. Clint would hate that! She was torn between resentment toward Valerie for even suggesting that he leave his beloved ranch—for not having the common sense to realize how much that ranch was a part of who he was, how it had helped form his personality—and disappointment with Clint for allowing himself to be talked into turning his back on his heritage.

* * *

Although Shannon had been sure, at the time of Clint's marriage, that she would die of a broken heart, eventually she was able to look at the situation from a philosophical point of view. He belonged to someone else now, and that was that.

By the time she went away to college she'd managed to put most of the hurt behind her—or at least bury it. It still surfaced now and then, however, such as when her mother relayed the news that a baby had been born to the young couple, a little girl they'd named Bethany.

Evelyn Gallagher is so thrilled, her mother wrote. *Every time she drops by she has new pictures of her grandchild.*

Thoughts of a baby girl with Clint's serious dark eyes brought about Shannon's determination, as nothing else could, that it was time to put all thoughts of Clint out of her mind and start building a new life.

It wasn't easy—for as long as she could remember, her dreams for the future had included Clint—but she knew she couldn't go on pining for something that could never be. She jumped wholeheartedly into campus activities, reasoning that if she kept herself busy enough she wouldn't have time to think about Clint. And when she moved to Seattle, shortly after graduation, she set about making friends and creating a busy social life for herself.

So far, though, she hadn't found that "someone else" Clint had assured her she would meet. She'd made an honest effort to give the men she knew a fair chance, but nobody had lived up to the image of Clint she carried in her memory.

For instance, there was Paul Foster, who was more

than just her employer. He was also her good friend. He'd waited several months after she came to work for him before asking her for a date, as if he didn't want to exploit his position as her boss. Eventually he had gotten around to asking her to go out with him, and they'd been dating casually—at least, it was casual on her part—since then. She was quite content with their friendly, easygoing relationship. Lately, though, he'd been hinting that he was ready for a more serious commitment, and the idea filled her with something close to panic.

She didn't want to give him false hopes, so she'd been skirting the issue. She knew it wasn't fair to keep him at arm's length indefinitely, however. He was too nice a guy for that. . . .

Her thoughts were interrupted by a voice calling, "Shannon! Shannon McCrae!" She turned to see a young woman about her own age rushing to catch up with her.

"Shannon, I thought that was you. I heard you were back in town."

"Terri Wells!" Shannon exclaimed. "It's great to see you!"

"How's your dad coming along?" Terri asked, after the two had embraced with enthusiasm. Just about everyone in Liberty had heard about the mishap that had befallen John McCrae while he was haying. He'd accidentally put the tractor in gear, and then had lost his balance and fallen off when it lurched forward. Before he'd been able to roll out of the way the tractor had run over his leg.

"He's getting more cantankerous by the day, so that must be a sign he's recovering," Shannon said. "He's not used to being inactive, and he's making life miserable for everyone around him. And then too, he's angry with himself for letting an accident like that happen in the first place.''

Terri grinned understandingly. Having lived all her life in this section of eastern Montana, she was aware that Shannon's father was one of that breed of tough, independent males common to the area. They considered themselves almost invincible, and impervious to the hazards ordinary mortals fall prey to.

"He *will* recover, won't he?" she asked.

"Oh yes, in time. You know what a tough old bird my dad is. He'll probably have a permanent limp—his leg was fractured in several places—but as long as he can climb back on a horse he'll be satisfied.''

"Are you back for good?"

"No, I still have my job waiting for me in Seattle. My boss was very sweet about telling me to take as much time as I need. Of course, the fact that I've worked through my last two vacations because we were so busy had a lot to do with it—he knows he owes me a favor or two. I've sublet my apartment, so I can stay as long as Mom needs me.''

As they were talking, Terri had fallen into step beside Shannon. When they reached the corner she said, "Well, this is as far as I go. I'm sure glad I ran into you. I hope we can spend some time together while you're here—or will you be too busy out at the ranch?''

"Oh, I'll have some free time. Sam Buckley is a good, dependable foreman, and we have a great crew. And Mom could run the ranch by herself if she had to—she knows as much about ranching as Dad. The main reason I came back is because I know she needs my moral and emotional support right now. This has been almost as hard on her as it has on Dad.''

''I can imagine. Listen, be sure and say hi to your folks for me.''

The two women parted after making plans to get together very soon to talk over old times, and Shannon continued down the street to the hardware store, where she was to pick up some items for their foreman. The brief encounter with Terri had lifted her spirits. Being welcomed so enthusiastically had given her a real sense of homecoming.

It *was* good to be back, and she was looking forward to renewing many old friendships. Except for a few brief trips she'd made to see her parents, she'd hardly been home at all since her graduation from college. Glancing around at the little town which was so dear and familiar to her, she found herself wondering how she could have stayed away so long.

But she knew the answer to that. When she was in her last year of college Clint's father had died suddenly, of a heart attack, and his mother, unwilling to take on the task of running the ranch by herself, had decided to go live with a sister in a neighboring state. That meant, of course, it was time for Clint to come back and take over. The only other alternative would have been to sell the place, which would be unthinkable. It had been in the family for generations.

Shannon had had every intention of returning to her hometown after graduation, but when the time came she found herself having second thoughts. All through college she'd been telling herself she had her feelings for Clint well under control, that she'd accepted the fact that he belonged to another woman.

From a distance it had been easy to be philosophical about his marriage to someone else. As graduation approached, though, she wasn't sure she could bear the strain of seeing him with Valerie day after day, of constantly having to be on her guard against doing or saying anything that would give away the truth—that she was still in love with him.

So, in spite of her yearning to return to where her roots lay, she'd headed toward the west coast, citing "better career opportunities" as her reason. If her parents had suspected her real motive, they'd tactfully refrained from commenting. Her job search had eventually taken her to Seattle, that sprawling city that lay between the sparkling waters of Puget Sound and the rugged Cascade Mountain range. Armed with her degree in computer science, she was soon hired by one of the many electronics companies that abounded in the Seattle area.

After a time she'd become restless working for the large, impersonal corporation, however, and felt that her creativity was being stifled. Looking for something more in keeping with her training and abilities, she'd gone to work for Paul Foster at *Software Specialties*, a small but prestigious company that supplied individualized computer programs for businesses. Her duties there were varied and challenging, and the fast pace of working for a business that was just getting started was exactly what she needed to take her mind off—other things. She threw herself into her new job, putting all her energy into doing her part to make the fledgling company a success.

Most of the time she was able to convince herself this was exactly what she wanted—to see more of the world than one small corner of Montana, to have an interesting career—and she was completely satisfied with the life she had chosen for herself.

Occasionally, though, when memories of all she'd left behind—not just Clint, but her parents, the ranch, the friends she'd grown up with—threatened to overwhelm her, little voice in the back of her mind asked, *Who do you think you're kidding?*

There had been one period when the yearning was so strong she was almost ready to pack it in and return home. Even living so close to Clint and knowing he'd never belong to her was preferable to being so far from all that mattered to her. And she'd reasoned that the knowledge that Clint was a happily married family man would quell any romantic notions she had toward him.

But then, just as she was seriously considering turning in her resignation and heading back to Montana, she learned that Clint's wife had left him. This bit of information put the whole situation in a different light.

Valerie never took to ranch life, Shannon's mother wrote, *but I never thought she'd abandon her husband and child that way. I feel so sorry for that poor little motherless girl.*

This new turn of affairs put Shannon in an awkward position. She was aware that if she came home now she might look awfully . . . well, *desperate.* She didn't want anyone—least of all Clint himself—to get the idea she'd come running back as soon as she heard he was available.

Later, when her mother wrote that they'd heard Valerie had died in a car accident, the situation still hadn't altered. Shannon would still appear to be chasing him if she returned. Anyway, her mother had said that Clint was different now, that he had become almost reclusive.

Shannon told herself she would probably be better off just staying in Seattle, safely away from Clint, at least until she reached a point where she could keep her feelings for him from being too obvious.

But then the matter was taken out of her hands by her father's accident. Her mother needed her now; she never even considered *not* returning home to offer her support.

Shannon was so caught up in her thoughts that she didn't notice she'd reached Jake Ledbetter's hardware store until she almost bumped into something stacked up outside the entrance. Catching herself just in time, she made her way around the display of lawn care items. She'd already embarrassed herself once this morning trying to avoid an encounter with Clint. Tripping over a sack of fertilizer and sprawling headfirst into a wheelbarrow because she was thinking about him rather than about where she was going would be the perfect encore performance.

As she entered the store she fished in her pocket for the list Sam had given her. Scanning it, she forced her thoughts back to the business at hand. Nails, paint, brushes, 12-2 wire, and an assortment of items to be used in repairing the pump. Starting at the top of the list, she headed toward the circular display bin where the nails, separated according to size, were sold by the pound. A scoop was provided, and a scale was suspended above the bin.

She was vaguely aware of the hum of voices and activity in the background. Customers came and went, calling out greetings to Jake and to one another. They made small talk about local gossip, the weather, and cattle prices while making their purchases. The voices blended together as Shannon concentrated on the items on Sam's list.

Without warning, a familiar, rich, masculine tone separated itself from the other sounds and penetrated her consciousness with startling clarity. Even though she hadn't heard it for ten years, that deep-timbred voice of Clint's was as well known to her as his face. And it still had the same devastating effect on her. Hearing it unexpectedly that way sent such a shock wave through her that her hand shook as she was lifting a scoop of nails.

In that split second before she regained her poise, the scoop, with its heavy burden, tilted downward. She stood frozen as the nails cascaded to the floor with a clatter that would have awakened the dead.

"Havin' some trouble?" Jake called out, as every eye in the store turned toward the source of the racket.

"No, I—I guess I'm just having an attack of the clumsies," she replied, attempting to make light of her predicament.

"As soon as I finish here I'll come back and give you a hand," Jake said.

"There's no need to. I'll handle it. You go ahead and take care of your customers."

With that she dropped to her knees and began picking up nails, hoping everyone would just forget about her and go on about their business. She blinked back tears of frustration. Was this the way it was going to be whenever she was anywhere near Clint? Was she going to fall apart every time he was in the vicinity?

She was aware that someone else—probably the high school boy who worked part-time for Jake—had knelt down and was helping gather up the spilled nails. She didn't want anyone to feel obligated to help her clean up the mess. It was embarrassing enough that she had caused such a commotion. "You don't have to ..." she started to murmur, stretching to retrieve several nails that had rolled almost out of her reach. Her words trailed off as she glanced up and found herself looking into Clint's deep brown eyes.

All at once her heart slammed against her ribs with such force that she felt suddenly light-headed. It crossed her mind, briefly, that it was a good thing she was kneeling on the floor, since she doubted if her legs could have supported her. Her bones had taken on the consistency of warm candle wax.

Her first thought—once her thought processes began to function again—was that all her innermost fantasies had suddenly taken on form and substance. Clint was right here in front of her, so close she could reach out and trace a finger along his lips, the line of his jaw. ...

If she had the courage to do such a thing, that was. The question was strictly academic anyway, since she seemed to have been frozen into immobility. At that moment, she couldn't have moved a muscle if her life depended on it.

Coming face-to-face with him this way, with no warning, had brought all the old feelings rushing back. In a split second of almost blinding revelation, it hit her that—no matter how she'd tried to deny it to herself—the love she'd felt for him ten years ago hadn't diminished one iota. If anything, it had become stronger.

Close on the heels of that thought came the realization that he didn't seem very pleased to see her. His expression was guarded, almost wary.

Was he afraid she was going to throw herself at him again, the way she had when she was sixteen? He needn't worry, she thought with a sudden surge of something close to resentment. She was a woman now, not a love-struck teenager, and nothing in the world would induce her to make that same mistake. She had bared her innermost emotions to him, and what had she gotten for it?

Just as if it had happened yesterday instead of ten years ago, all the hurt and humiliation of his long-ago rejection came rushing back with such force that it was almost a physical blow.

The painful memory jarred her out of her momentary paralysis. She couldn't just keep staring at him, as if she'd suddenly been stricken mute. Instinctively, she drew a deep, steadying breath of air into her lungs.

"Hello, Clint," she got out. She was surprised at how composed she sounded, when her world had suddenly been turned upside down.

"Shannon," Clint replied, touching the brim of his hat in a brief gesture that could have meant almost anything. "I heard you were back."

She tried to ignore the fact that even his voice still had the power to send a tingling weakness through her. "Yes . . . ah, came back as soon as I heard about Dad's accident."

He nodded, as if acknowledging that, of course, she couldn't have done otherwise.

She swallowed hard, her throat dry as dust. Forcing movement into her limbs, she reached out to finish picking up the spilled nails. When her fingers accidentally touched his she drew her hand back, but not before the brief contact sent a jolt of electricity all the way up her arm. If Clint was similarly affected he was keeping it well hidden, Shannon thought. Nothing in his expression revealed any hint of his feelings.

Gathering up the last few nails, Clint straightened and carefully placed the scoop back in the bin, then held his hand out to Shannon to help her up. She pretended not to notice it as she slowly and methodically brushed the dust from her hands. With the unexpected encounter already having such a disastrous effect on her, she didn't dare trust her reaction if she were to place her hand in his. She gave her palms a final wipe on the legs of her jeans, and scrambled to her feet unassisted.

Standing, he seemed even taller than she remembered—and overwhelmingly male. She took a step backward when she realized she was so close to him she could almost feel the heat from his body.

With a determined effort of will, she pulled what was left of her poise around her like a protective garment. "Well, ah, thanks for your help," she murmured as she carefully poured the scoop of nails into one of the paper bags provided. She wasn't even sure if these were the kind of nails Sam had specified. At this moment, they could have been carpet tacks or railroad spikes, for all she cared, as long as she had something to do to keep her hands from shaking.

"No problem," Clint replied in an impersonal tone. He touched the brim of his hat again.

Shannon felt something more was called for, but all the polite, conventional phrases escaped her for the moment. The silence between them lengthened, until Clint finally asked, "How long are you planning to be here?"

"I'm not sure," she replied vaguely. "It just depends on how long Mom needs me."

Clint shifted his weight from one foot to the other. "Well then, ah, I guess I'll be seeing you around."

"Uh-huh. I suppose so."

That seemed to exhaust all the possible conversational avenues. She knew it was ridiculous that she couldn't think of a thing to say to Clint, whom she'd known all her life, but his demeanor didn't invite small talk. As her mother had said, he'd changed. She grabbed up the bag of nails without bothering to weigh them. With a murmured, "I-I'd better get on with my shopping," she made a hasty retreat toward another section of the store.

As exit lines went, it wouldn't win any prizes. She had to put some distance between herself and Clint, though, before she made an even bigger fool of herself.

Clint watched as she walked away, admiring her long, slim, denim-clad legs and the way her jeans molded her shapely hips. The promise that had been evident when she was a teenager had been fulfilled. She had grown into a beautiful woman.

Running into her like this had caught him completely off guard. When he'd heard the clatter of nails he'd automatically bent down to lend a hand. Finding himself face-to-face with this new, grown-up version of his old childhood friend had rendered him momentarily speechless. A multitude of thoughts and impressions had tumbled through his mind: the auburn hair that fell over one side of her face in a thick, lustrous curtain; the jade-green eyes opened wide in surprise; the lips, soft and full, faintly pink . . .

He shook his head to clear away the image. Thank goodness she was only going to be around for a short time. He'd have to make a point of staying out of her way while she was here. She was much too attractive. A woman like that could make a man start having ideas that could only lead to trouble.

Still, he'd known her all his life, and he could have shown a *little* more warmth at seeing her again, his conscience nagged at him. *Nice going, Gallagher,* he berated himself. He hadn't seen her in ten years, and the best he could do was, "I guess I'll be seeing you around." Had there been just a hint of hurt in her expression?

He wondered briefly if he was destined to go through life causing her distress. Something twisted inside him as he recalled the look in her eyes when he'd told her there could never be anything between them but friendship, that she was too young to know her own mind, that someday she'd meet someone else. . . .

He winced now, at the thought of how insufferably arrogant he must have sounded.

He hadn't wanted to hurt her that way, but he didn't see what else he could have done. What kind of guy would he have been if he'd allowed her to go on believing that she was really in love with him? She'd been just a kid, he reminded himself, too young to know her own mind.

But she wasn't a kid now—and that realization filled him with an inexplicable uneasiness.

Chapter Two

Shaken by the encounter with Clint, Shannon rushed through the rest of her shopping as quickly as possible. A brief stop at the grocery store, and then she was headed home. At least she hadn't run into Clint in the market. If she had, there was no telling what kind of havoc she might have wreaked. She couldn't help smiling a little at the image of herself leaving a trail of broken jars and dented cans in her wake. No doubt about it—she simply had to get herself under control.

By the time she pulled into the driveway and parked, she'd managed to recover her poise. All the way home she'd lectured herself about how she *was* going to be meeting Clint frequently, so she may as well get used to it. She'd always considered herself a more or less "together" person. There was no reason why she should go into a tailspin every time he was in the vicinity.

Having given herself this little pep talk, she felt certain that the next time she came face-to-face with Clint she would be able to conduct herself with a certain amount of decorum.

As she carried her groceries toward the house she could hear her father's rumbling voice. Deep and resonant, it floated out through the open windows and across the lawn. ''What about that hay that's already been baled? It has to be brought into the barn soon. What if it rains? It'll be ruined.''

''It'll get done,'' Shannon's mother Maureen was saying, in a tone that indicated a tenuous grip on her patience. ''Sam will see to it. That's what we pay him for.''

The double doors to the study just off the living room were open. As Shannon entered the house she saw that her mother was at the desk going over some paperwork, while her father propelled his wheelchair back and forth across one end of the room.

''For heaven's sake, will you stop pacing?'' Maureen said.

''I'm not pacing,'' John McCrae shot back testily. ''According to the dictionary, 'pace' means 'to walk back and forth.' How can a man pace when he's in a wheelchair?''

Shannon smiled. It was hard to tell whether her father's enforced inactivity was harder on him or her mother. Thank goodness Dr. Haines had promised him a walking cast next week. Once he was able to get around a little more, maybe he'd stop trying to browbeat everyone within earshot.

''If that pump isn't repaired before the dry season we're going to be in big trouble,'' John grumbled. ''What if we have a drought, like we did a few years ago?''

''Calm down.'' Maureen's voice rose slightly. ''First you worry that it'll rain, and then you worry that it *won't*.''

''Sam knows the pump needs to be repaired,''

Shannon said, glancing into the room. "He gave me a list of parts for it. They're out in the truck."

"Hello, dear," her mother greeted her as she looked up from her paperwork. "Let me help you put those groceries away."

"That's all right. I can manage. I see you're busy."

"I *insist*," Maureen replied, jumping up quickly. Shannon's protest died on her lips as she realized her mother sounded almost—well, desperate.

"Somebody better remember to get down to the south pasture and check on that fence." John's voice followed Shannon and her mother as they went down the hall to the kitchen. "If it isn't done before the herd is moved we could have cattle straying all over the county."

Maureen rolled her eyes toward the ceiling, as if petitioning the heavens for strength. "I don't see how anyone could forget," she called back. "I'm sure everyone on the ranch can hear you ranting and raving." Under her breath she said, through clenched teeth, "He's driving me stark, raving mad!"

"Cheer up. He'll be easier to get along with once he can get out of his wheelchair."

"If I let him live that long," Maureen murmured.

Shannon knew the situation wasn't as serious as it sounded. Her parents were as much in love as they'd been when they'd married thirty years ago. Her father always grumbled when he was frustrated, and her mother always complained about his temper. They'd weathered other storms, and Shannon was sure they'd get through this one.

"Maybe he'll calm down when Clint gets here and

he has another man to talk to,'' Maureen said as she unloaded grocery bags.

Shannon looked up from her kneeling position, where she was putting canned goods in a lower cupboard. "Clint is coming *here?*"

"Yes, didn't I mention that? He and your father are making plans to irrigate that strip of land between our ranch and the Gallagher place, and they need to iron out the details. You sound surprised."

"I—I just . . . from your letters I got the idea he keeps pretty much to himself."

"Oh, that. He's all right around your father and me—he's known us all his life, for goodness' sake. What I meant was that he never attends social events—parties and barn dances, that sort of thing," Maureen explained. "And he doesn't date, even though, heaven knows, he's certainly had enough chances—or did, before all the eligible women around here gave up on him."

She shook her head. "He should be looking for a mother for his daughter. Not that he isn't a good father—even if he *is* somewhat overprotective. I suppose that's natural for a man raising a little girl." She neatly folded the grocery bag she had just emptied, and placed it in a rack under the sink.

"A child that age needs a mother, though," she went on. "His housekeeper, Thelma, does the best she can—you remember Thelma Kruger, don't you?—and she's very fond of Bethany, but she's not a young woman anymore, and it's hard for her to keep up with an active child."

"What's his daughter like?" Shannon couldn't help asking.

"Oh, she's an adorable child—big dark eyes and long thick hair."

Shannon has a quick image of a little girl with Clint's deep brown eyes. She couldn't suppress the little pang of wistfulness that shot through her. At one time she'd taken it for granted that someday *she'd* be the mother of Clint's children. She pushed the thought from her mind.

"More than one woman around here decided he'd be a good catch, after Valerie left him," Maureen remarked thoughtfully, "but he never paid any attention to any of them, and after a while they all quit trying. I can't say I blame them—he became so grim and unapproachable he probably scared them all off. A woman would have to care an awful lot about a man to put up with . . ." Her voice trailed off as she looked at her daughter speculatively.

Shannon finished putting the cans away, then stood up and started on the refrigerator items. "Do you want me to leave the lettuce and tomatoes out so we can have a salad for dinner?" she asked, her head inside the refrigerator.

"Um . . . yes, why don't you." Maureen carried the vegetables to the sink and began to wash them. "You know, I really hate to see Clint shut himself away like that," she commented.

Shannon closed the refrigerator door and shot a glance at her mother, but Maureen's back was to her. Her tone revealed nothing except a casual interest in their longtime neighbor.

"He used to be so outgoing and easy to get along with, even when he was just a boy," Maureen went on. "Remember how he never even minded the way you used to tag along after him when you were a child?''

As if I could ever forget, Shannon thought. Looking back, she was sure she must have made a horrible pest of herself. She'd been too young at the time to realize how embarrassing it might have been to him, having the little neighbor girl constantly dogging his footsteps. Yet he'd never indicated, by so much as an irritated glance, that he wished she'd just go away and stop bothering him. He'd been patience itself, teaching her to ride, answering her many questions. But patience hadn't been enough to close that six-year gap between them. She recalled the time her mother had found her in tears because Clint was getting ready to go away to college.

''I know you think the world of Clint, but you have to realize he's becoming a young man now, and you're still a little girl,'' her mother had explained gently.

''B-but he's not supposed to grow up without me,'' the twelve-year-old Shannon had sobbed. ''He's supposed to wait for me.''

Now her cheeks flamed at the memory. She began putting boxes in one of the upper cupboards, with quick, businesslike movements. ''I see I didn't need to buy cookies,'' she commented. ''There are already two unopened boxes up there. I suppose they'll get eaten, though. I remember Dad always liked those kind with the frosting in the middle.'' She realized she was rambling, but she was doing her best to divert the conversation from the subject of Clint Gallagher. Her mother was entirely too observant sometimes.

* * *

Driving home, Clint tried to shake the uneasy feeling he'd had ever since his surprise encounter with Shannon. He told himself that unexpected rush of— he wasn't sure what to call it; wistful yearning?—that had almost overwhelmed him was simply the normal reaction of any man toward an attractive woman. *Don't get any ideas,* a voice in the back of his mind said.

Although whatever he'd once felt for Valerie had died a long time ago, the lesson he'd learned remained with him. He'd made one serious mistake by becoming involved with a woman who preferred the city to ranch life. His only excuse was that he'd been so bedazzled that his common sense had deserted him. He'd been young then, and naive, and Valerie, a tanned, golden, southern California girl, had represented a whole new world to him.

In the first flush of what he'd thought was love— but which he now knew had been merely infatuation— he'd even allowed her to talk him into leaving his beloved ranch to start their married life in Los Angeles. The agreement had been that they would live there, and he would work for Valerie's uncle, until his father was ready to retire. Then they would return so he could take over running the ranch.

When the time came, though, and they had taken up residence at the ranch, it soon became obvious that Valerie had no intention of settling down to be a rancher's wife. When her tears and pleading couldn't convince him to change his mind and move back to Los Angeles, she'd simply said she was going, with or without him. By then, realizing what a disaster his marriage was, he cared little whether she left or not.

He'd put his foot down, though, at her taking Bethany along. He didn't intend to allow his daughter to grow up as spoiled and shallow as her mother. Whether Valerie realized she couldn't win if it came down to a court battle, or if she simply decided it wasn't worth the effort, she gave in and let him have custody.

The whole affair had left him wary and distrustful of women, and he'd carefully schooled himself to put any stray romantic notions out of his mind. He'd concentrated all his time and energies into running his ranch and raising his daughter—the only good thing that had come of the whole affair.

Even if he *were* inclined to seek out a relationship, it certainly wouldn't be with another woman who disliked ranch life—and Shannon obviously fell into that category. Otherwise she wouldn't have gone off to Seattle as soon as she was out of college, and made her home there.

That didn't mean, however, that seeing her again hadn't caused a restless stirring inside him. After all, she'd matured into a beautiful woman. He had better sense than to make the same mistake twice, though. Now that he was aware of the effect she had on him, the wisest thing he could do would be to stay as far away from her as possible while she was here.

He recalled, with dismay, that he had promised her father he'd drop by later today. He hoped he could slip into the study and talk to John there, and avoid running into Shannon at all. It wasn't likely she'd want to join them. He could assume she had little interest in ranch business. If she had, she wouldn't have moved so far away.

He couldn't suppress a slight resentment. John, and Maureen too, were among the few really close friends he had these days, and he looked forward to his occasional visits to the McCrae ranch. Now those visits wouldn't be the same if he had to skulk around, trying to keep from encountering Shannon.

He was about halfway home when he spotted the light-blue van bearing the logo *Rowena's Flowers* parked along the shoulder of the road. Clint pulled up behind the van and walked up to the window on the driver's side. Henry Stubing, the middle-aged deliveryman, was resting his chin on his hand and gazing out the window with a patient air.

"Thanks for stopping," Henry said, "but I've already sent word back to Rowena that the van broke down. There's a tow truck on the way."

"Since everything seems to be under control, I guess I'll be going on," Clint said, turning to leave.

"There is one thing you could do. I was on my way to take some flowers out to the McCrae place. In this heat I'm afraid they'll be wilted by the time I get towed into town and can get the other van. I hate to ask you to play deliveryman for a flower shop, but since you go right by there . . ."

Clint hesitated just slightly. If someone was sending flowers to Shannon, the last thing he wanted to do was deliver them. He reminded himself that the flowers weren't necessarily for her, that John could have ordered them for Maureen. Deep inside he knew how unlikely that was, though. If John wanted to make a romantic gesture, he'd be more inclined to buy his wife a new saddle, or a pair of riding boots.

He saw that Henry was looking at him expectantly,

and he didn't see how he could gracefully refuse the request, especially since he was planning to stop by the McCrae place anyway. "Sure, I'll drop them off for you," he heard himself saying.

Henry smiled his thanks, and got out to open the back door of the van. "I sure appreciate this," he said as the arrangement of deep-red roses was being transferred to the front seat of Clint's pickup truck. "Some guy called all the way from Seattle to order these." Clearly, he was impressed by this gesture. "Wouldn't look good for the shop if we delivered wilted flowers. Well, I sure thank you for your help."

"No problem," Clint replied, climbing back into his pickup. Although he kept his tone expressionless, he felt as if he'd been doused with icy water.

As he continued on his way he glanced over at the roses and scowled. It was next to impossible to ignore them, with their heady scent filling the cab of the truck. He couldn't say just why the sight of them irritated him so. It was none of his business that some guy in Seattle was sending roses to Shannon.

Still, he couldn't keep his mind from conjuring up an image of this unknown suitor of hers. The picture that came to mind was of a smooth-talking character in a three-piece suit, with a toothy smile and soft, uncallused hands. What could she possibly see in a guy like that? The Shannon he remembered was vivacious and dynamic; she had a zest for life. He had a brief vision of her as a teenager, riding her little mare in a barrel race at a local rodeo, her color high with the excitement of competition.

Another image crowded in, of Shannon at her sixteenth birthday party. She'd worn some kind of white off-the-shoulder peasant dress that accentuated her deep tan and cloud of auburn hair. He recalled how the clinging material had emphasized the maturing curves of her soft young body, and the light that had shone in her eyes every time she'd looked his way. . . .

. . . and the way that light had faded when he'd told her there could never be anything between them except friendship.

He shook his head to clear away the unwelcome memories.

Shannon was still up on the step stool putting away the last of the groceries when she glanced out the window and saw Clint's pickup pulling into the driveway. She resisted the urge to run into her room to comb her hair and dab on some lipstick. He was coming to see her father, she reminded herself. Still, she couldn't help the little tingle of excitement as she heard his footsteps on the back porch. She knew that would be him—hardly anyone around here came to the front door, except strangers who were lost and needed directions.

"C'mon in," she called through the screen door, wondering why he didn't just push it open and come in, as he used to do. After all, he'd been running in and out of the McCrae house ever since he was a boy.

Shannon couldn't hear all of his reply, but it sounded something like, ". . . got my hands full . . ." She climbed down from the step stool and went to admit him.

"Ah—these are for you—"

As she held the door open, he thrust the flowers toward her as if he were anxious to be rid of them.

A warm glow of pleasure spread through Shannon as she accepted the armload of roses, although she was somewhat taken aback by Clint's unique method of presenting them. But, so what if he didn't have a pretty speech prepared to go with them? It was the thought that counted, wasn't it?

She wondered what had possessed him to bring her flowers. Were they meant as a peace offering, to make up for his rather cool greeting in the hardware store? She reminded herself they needn't signify anything except maybe "Welcome home." Still, that was better than nothing.

"How thoughtful of you to bring these," she exclaimed. She laid them on the counter and extracted the white envelope nestled among the velvety petals.

Clint shrugged self-consciously. "I don't know if I'd exactly call it 'thoughtful.' All I did was deliver them for Henry Stubing when the flower shop van broke down up on the highway. I was headed this way anyhow, so it wouldn't have seemed neighborly not to."

As Clint's words sank in, Shannon could feel a flush rising all the way to the roots of her hair. How could she have been so foolish as to think Clint would bring her flowers? It was bad enough that she'd gushed about him being "thoughtful," but thank goodness she hadn't revealed that she'd thought the roses were from him. "Of course. I—I just meant it was thoughtful of you to do a favor for Henry."

With trembling fingers she opened the envelope and glanced at the brief message on the card. It read:

Shannon—
   You can't imagine how much I miss you. I'm counting the days until your return.
                          —All my love, Paul

She tucked the card into her shirt pocket. She couldn't help wondering if Clint was at all curious about who the flowers were from—possibly even a bit jealous? But that was just wishful thinking, she told herself.

"Oh, hello, Clint," her mother said, coming into the kitchen. "I thought I heard you drive up . . ." Her voice trailed off as she spotted the roses. "Did somebody around here just win the Kentucky Derby?"

"They're for me," Shannon told her. "From . . . from my employer. He, ah, he just wanted to let me know he misses . . . he misses my work," Shannon explained, wishing there were some way she could convey to her mother, *Don't make a big deal out of this.* "Clint was kind enough to bring them out when Henry's van broke down."

"Oh." Maureen seemed to recognize her daughter's unspoken plea. "John is waiting for you in the study, Clint," she said briskly. "He'll be glad to have company."

"That you, Clint?" John's voice came from down the hallway. "C'mon in here. I need a man to talk to. These women treat me like some kind of invalid."

As Clint started to leave the room, Maureen said, "You will stay for supper, won't you?"

"Well . . ." Clint hesitated.

Oh, no, Shannon thought. Still embarrassed over her mistaken assumption that the flowers were from Clint, she had no desire to sit across a table from him and have to make polite conversation.

This time her mother didn't appear to be so perceptive, however. "I happen to know Thelma took Bethany over to Barston this afternoon to do some serious clothes shopping, and they're not planning to be back until evening, so there's no reason for you to rush home. I'll set a place for you."

Shannon couldn't help noticing Clint's expression. It was obvious he wasn't any happier about this turn of events than she was.

John and Clint were still talking ranch business when Maureen called them to come to the table. "Well, well. What's the occasion?" John asked as he wheeled himself through the living room, where the roses, displayed on a low table, seemed to dominate the room. Actually, Shannon would have preferred to put them in a less prominent spot—*Like the attic,* she thought wryly—but hiding them away would only have drawn more attention to them. It made her uncomfortable that Paul had sent such a blatant symbol of his feelings for her. She didn't want her parents—and yes, Clint, she admitted—to get the idea she was seriously involved with him.

"My employer sent them," she told her father. She hoped he would grasp, from her tone, that she would rather not discuss the matter.

John didn't seem to get her message, though. "Your employer, huh?" He raised his eyebrows.

"He, ah, he's a good friend, too," she explained lamely.

"Oh, so that's how it is."

Shannon wanted to insist, *No, that's not how it is,* but she decided the less said about the whole thing, the better.

"One of these days some man is going to come along and marry my girl," John went on, shaking his head. "I guess I'd better get used to the idea. I always hoped it would be someone from around here, though, and not some city slicker."

Shannon felt her cheeks growing warm. She stole a glance at Clint, but it was impossible to tell what he was thinking. His face had that same closed expression she'd noticed when she'd seen him walking down the street.

"Everything's on the table," Maureen said, breaking the sudden silence. "Let's sit down and eat while it's hot."

During the meal, Shannon felt as if she'd turned invisible. Clint directed most of his conversation toward her parents. It was just as well, she thought. If she kept her mouth shut she would be less likely to blurt out something that would give away her feelings toward him—the feelings she'd thought were dead and buried, but which she now had to admit were just as strong as ever. And it didn't help that the scent of those roses wafted into the room, reminding her of how delighted she'd been when she'd thought Clint had cared enough to bring her flowers.

She could see she was really going to have to watch herself when she was around him. She'd humiliated herself ten years ago by revealing how she felt about him. She wasn't going to let that happen again. . . .

She was brought sharply back from her memories by the realization that her father had asked her something.

"What?" She forced her attention back to the present.

"I was just saying, now that you've had your fling at life in the fast lane isn't it about time you gave some thought to coming back home where you belong?"

She knew he was only half serious. They had some variation of this discussion every time she came home for a visit. Although he was pleased that she had a career and could take care of herself, he seemed to feel a fatherly obligation to try to talk her into moving back to Liberty. "Now, Dad," she began, "we've already been through this—"

"Oh, I don't mean I expect you to live here on the ranch again. I realize you're an adult, with your own life to lead, but you could get an apartment in town. That way we'd at least get to see you more than just at Thanksgiving and Christmas."

"And what about my job? I do have to make a living," she reminded him with a little smile.

He brushed aside that argument with a wave of his hand. "There are a lot of places around here that use computers. Or you could start up your own business, as a"—he searched for the right term—"a computer consultant," he finished triumphantly.

In spite of her protests, she had to admit the idea was appealing. Just being back for a little while had made her realize this was where she longed to be. There was only one thing keeping her from giving serious consideration to her father's suggestion. Being so close to Clint, and having to guard her every word to keep from giving away her feelings toward him, would be too much of a strain.

She managed a smile. "You know I love living in Seattle. And I'm on my way up in the company."

John spread his hands in a gesture of helplessness. "You try to do right by your kids and see that they get a good education, and what do they do? Run off and desert you in your old age."

Shannon rolled her eyes heavenward. He always managed to throw in a reference to his "old age," although, at fifty, he was as fit and active as most men half his age—or was, until his accident forced him to slow down. And he would be again, once his injured leg was healed.

"It's your fault, you know," she countered, keeping her voice light. "You raised me to be independent."

Her father gave an exaggerated sigh. "What did I do to deserve such an ungrateful child?"

It was obvious, from his wink and the twinkle in his eye, that he was only teasing. Still, she would rather not have this conversation in front of Clint. She wondered what his reaction was to her assertion that she preferred city life and a career to moving back here where she'd been raised. Was he likening her to his ex-wife?

Considering Clint's broken marriage, and the reasons for it, she felt a change of subject was in order. She tried to think of some way to communicate this to her father.

It was too late, though. Turning to Clint, John shook his head in mock despair. "Can you imagine anyone in their right mind preferring city life to living on a ranch?''

Clint was silent for several moments, as if weighing his reply. Just when it seemed he wasn't going to answer, he said, "It seems to me a person who is happier in the city ought to just stay there, It's easier on everyone." His words, like flat, heavy stones, made the others at the table look at him curiously.

In the sudden, uncomfortable silence, John's expression seemed to be asking, *Hey, did I say something wrong?* Although Shannon loved her father dearly, sometimes he wasn't too quick on the uptake, she thought, especially when it came to picking up on such subtleties as nuances and undertones. She realized she'd better say something quickly, before her father opened his mouth again and said something to make the situation worse.

"I hear you're planning to irrigate that strip of land down by the south pasture. Are you going to use it for grazing land, or plant hay?"

John brightened, as he always did when he had a chance to talk ranching. "I thought we could put hay in the upper section, and fence off the lower part and use it for a summer pasture. . . .''

As he outlined his plans for the strip of land, Shannon stole a glance at Clint out of the corner of her eye, but his expression was unreadable. If she had to describe it, she'd have to say it seemed to be a curious mixture of relief and disapproval.

Chapter Three

"There, there, it's going to be all right," Shannon crooned, slipping a rope around the calf, just behind its front legs, and tying it securely. Her tone was soothing as she tried to calm the frightened creature, who gazed up at her and bawled forlornly.

While she was out checking fences she'd come upon the animal, mired fast in a mud hole. Judging from the way the wet, slushy ground around him was churned up, he'd been there for quite a while. His struggles to free himself had only served to drive his back legs deeper into the mud.

Now he seemed to have all but given up. At her approach he'd given a few halfhearted kicks with his front legs, obviously summoning the last of his strength.

Satisfied that the rope was tied securely, Shannon hurried back to the mare, Lucy, who was standing by patiently. Fitting a toe into the stirrup, she swung herself into the saddle and wound the other end of the rope around the pommel. With a light touch on the reins and gentle knee pressure, she urged the horse a few steps backward.

"Good girl," she murmured, dismounting and running back to the mud hole. Struggling to keep her footing on the slippery ground, she placed one booted foot behind her for balance as she tugged on the rope. The mare, a veteran of many years of ranch work, seemed to know just what was expected of her. She braced her forelegs, keeping just the right amount of tension on the rope.

The calf bawled mournfully and rolled his eyes in fright as the rope began to tighten around him. "It's for your own good," Shannon muttered through clenched teeth. She continued pulling until she felt the slight "give" that told her her efforts were successful.

In a few minutes the calf had been pulled free, and lay panting on the dry ground. After a quick examination determined that he was uninjured, Shannon removed the rope and recoiled it. "Now then, I wonder where your mama is," she said, looking down at the exhausted calf.

Her question was answered almost immediately, as the mare's warning nicker and the sound of something moving through the thick brush alerted her. Whirling around, she found herself confronting a large and angry-looking cow—obviously the calf's mother. Head down, the animal glared at Shannon.

Uh-oh, a little voice in the back of Shannon's mind said. The look in the beast's eye boded no good for her. This wasn't the first time she'd faced an over-protective mother cow, and she knew how aggressive the normally placid creatures could be when they thought their young were threatened.

The cow's attention was diverted briefly by a sound from her baby, who was struggling to get to his feet. She glanced uncertainly from Shannon to the calf. The pull of motherhood apparently won out over a desire to assert herself, and she reluctantly turned to her off-spring.

Shannon was aware that the animal could still change her mind, though. With slow, cautious movements she began edging toward Lucy, keeping a wary eye on the cow as she did so. When she judged that she was close enough, she covered the last few feet in a run and swung into the saddle.

"Ingrate!" she called over her shoulder as she swung the mare around and nudged her into a gallop. "If you'd been looking after him like you should have, he wouldn't have gotten in trouble in the first place."

"I can't remember the last time I felt so exhausted," Shannon said to her mother as she came in the back door, after kicking her boots off outside and brushing away as much of the dried mud as she could. Going into the living room, she eased herself into the comfortable old blanket-covered chair her dad always relaxed in when he came in dirty and muddy.

She'd caught a glimpse of herself in the mirror over the fireplace, and she couldn't help smiling at the thought of what her friends in Seattle would say if they could see her now, her jeans and western shirt dirty and stained, her face devoid of makeup, her hair hanging in limp strands. She could well imagine their amusement, had they observed her up to her ankles in mud as she rescued a stranded calf or confronted its hostile mother.

Not that she'd *had* to spend her day in such pursuits, of course. Although an extra pair of hands was always welcome around a ranch, she knew her dad had a per-

fectly competent crew who could manage just fine
without her help. She'd pitched in because it was
something she liked to do. She'd grown up doing
ranch chores, and it gave her a satisfactory sense of
accomplishment to know she hadn't lost her touch.
Besides, in Seattle the only time she ever got a really
good workout was when she went to the health spa,
or jogging in Greenlake Park. In spite of her sore,
aching muscles, she'd enjoyed the vigorous exercise.

Her thoughts went back to the half-joking conversation she'd had with her dad at the dinner table a few
days ago, when he suggested she move back to Liberty. Although she knew she couldn't take that suggestion seriously, she couldn't help speculating on
what her life might be like if she did.

Giving her imagination free rein, she pictured herself spending weekends and days off at the ranch,
helping out during roundups, taking part in discussions
about the buying and selling of stock and equipment,
using her computer skills to keep track of finances and
other ranch business.

No matter how appealing the fantasy was, though,
she was aware that was all it could ever be—a fantasy.
With Clint living on the neighoring ranch it was all
but impossible for her to even consider moving back
home. Being so near him and knowing her feelings for
him would never be reciprocated would be too much
of a strain on her emotions. A chill went through her
at the memory of how cool he'd been toward her the
few times she'd encountered him since she'd been
back. . . .

She was jolted back to the present by the ringing of
the phone. Drawing a deep breath, she waited for the

image of Clint, his expression aloof and distant, to fade away, before picking up the phone.

"That you, Shannon?" a voice came over the line. "This is Walt Davies."

"Oh, hello, Walt. Just a minute. I'll go get Dad . . ."

"I didn't call to talk to John. You're the one I need to talk to."

Why in the world would Walt Davies be calling me? Shannon wondered. Walt, a local rancher, was a contemporary of her father's. "It's nice to hear from you, Walt."

Walt chuckled. "You might not think so when I tell you why I called. You know, don't you, I'm the current president of the Silver Spurs?"

"Yes, I remember hearing that." She was familiar, of course, with Silver Spurs, a local riding club. From the time she was eight until she was well into her teens, she'd been a member of the junior mounted drill team sponsored by the club. She waited for Walt to continue.

"I'll get right to the point. We're losing our drill team advisor, and your name came up when we were discussing who we could get as a replacement. After all the time you spent in drill team, you'd be perfect for the position. And you're young enough that you can relate to the kids."

When Shannon hesitated, he went on, "You wouldn't be expected to do it all by yourself, of course. The parents will look after the tack and costumes, and chaperone the kids when we go to out-of-town shows, but we need someone who can coach them in the drill movements."

"I'm flattered that you think I can handle it, but I'm only going to be here temporarily, you know," she replied.

"We realize that, but if you can just fill in until we find a permanent advisor, we'd sure appreciate it. The first competition of the season is coming up over in Fremont in three weeks. We have to find someone soon if the team is going to be ready."

When it was put to her that way, she couldn't come up with any good reason for not lending a hand, especially since she'd made up her mind to prolong her stay for a while longer. Although her dad was recovering nicely, she wasn't quite ready to leave just yet. She was enjoying her first real visit home in quite a while. She'd kept her nose to the grindstone for a long time—even working through several vacations while Paul was getting his fledgling company started—and now that the business was showing every sign of being a success, she was entitled to some time off.

She'd already told Paul, when he'd called the other evening to ask how her father was doing and when she was planning to come back, that she'd decided to extend her stay.

"I'm not trying to rush you," he'd said. "I know I told you to take as much time as you need. You have it coming to you. It's just that—well, I miss you."

That was another reason she was reluctant to go back, she admitted to herself, somewhat guiltily. The sooner she returned to Seattle, the sooner she'd have to deal with Paul. He'd been hinting that it was time their relationship took a more serious turn, and the idea filled her with panic. She didn't want to hurt him, but she wasn't ready to make a commitment. She wasn't sure she ever would be—to him or anyone else.

She'd tried to tell herself it was because she had to concentrate on her career. Deep down, though, she knew that wasn't the real reason. She'd already proven herself in her chosen field. The truth was, any man paled in comparison to Clint.

Was this what the rest of her life was going to be, she wondered—rejecting every man she met because nobody could measure up to the fantasy she'd built up in her mind? *I'll probably die an old maid,* she thought wryly. She could picture herself as an old lady, alone and unloved, still pining away for a love that could never be.

But whatever her motives for prolonging her stay, she'd found herself telling Walt, "I'll be glad to help out."

She felt completely at ease as she sat astride Lucy in the middle of the practice arena. The rhythmic pounding of hooves, the smells of horseflesh and saddle leather, even the gritty taste of the dust that almost obliterated the horses and their young riders, all blended together into a rich mixture of almost-forgotten sensations.

She watched with a practiced eye as the twenty-four riders guided their horses through the various movements that would eventually come together into a smooth, orderly pattern. Most of the kids had been in drill team for several years so they were familiar with the maneuvers, and the new members of the team seemed to be picking it up from the more experienced youngsters without too much trouble.

There was Bethany, for instance, the little girl with the long, wavy dark hair cascading down her back. Her delicate features were a study in concentration as she guided her small bay gelding through the movements.

The child had to be Clint's daughter—even if her last name hadn't been Gallagher, there was no mistaking those serious brown eyes or the firmness of that well-shaped mouth, in spite of its childish contours. She sat her horse well, Shannon noticed. Knees and elbows in, back straight, hands grasping the reins firmly.

Yes, Shannon had no doubt that Bethany would be an asset to the team. Of course, she couldn't become a member without the obligatory permission form signed by her father, but there was time enough for that. This was just the first day of practice. She'd have to remember to send the forms home with the kids at the end of today's session.

Shannon wheeled Lucy around and surveyed the circle of riders critically, looking for any weakness that would mar the smooth execution of the drill maneuvers. "Amy, close up that gap," she called out. "Brian, keep your horse's head up." A movement on the other side of the arena caught her eye and she rode across the ring to where Cody, another of the new members, was having some problems. She motioned for him to get out of line, calling to the leader as she did so, "Matt, circle the ring once more and then come up the center in columns of twos." She turned her attention to Cody, giving him a few tips for keeping his horse under control.

"Think you can handle it now?" she asked. He

nodded earnestly, and she watched as the others slowed down slightly so he could slip back into line.

By now the riders had started up the center of the ring, two by two. When they reached a certain point, mid-center, the columns veered off in opposite directions, each forming a circle. Shannon watched with satisfaction as the two groups separated, then merged again, this time in columns of four.

Her attention was diverted by a rider entering the ring at the far end. Even from this distance she could tell it was Clint. And for once she had no difficulty knowing what was on his mind. Everything about him indicated anger and disapproval.

She nudged Lucy into motion and made her way toward him, down the outside of the practice area. As she did so, she glanced over her shoulder at the young riders, who had just completed their maneuver and brought their horses to a halt, forming a single row that faced what would be the judges' stand if this were a competition. "Straighten out that line," she called, knowing how easily judges would be turned off by a straggly line.

As she turned her attention back to Clint, she could see that his face was like a thundercloud. His brows were drawn together and his mouth was set in a firm line. As if sensing its rider's mood, his horse tossed its head and danced nervously, but Clint's strong hands on the reins kept the powerful animal in check.

"Is—is something wrong?" Shannon asked as she approached him.

"You'd better believe something's wrong." He ground the words out. "What's my daughter doing here? I didn't give my permission for her to be in drill team.''

Although Shannon was taken aback by the force of his anger, she stifled the flash of resentment that surged through her at being spoken to in this manner. She'd already sensed that being a member of the team was important to Bethany, but she recalled her mother mentioning Clint's overprotectiveness toward the child. She reminded herself she would have to proceed carefully.

"The permission forms haven't been sent home yet," she explained in as calm a tone as she could manage. "I can give you one if you'd like, and you can sign it now."

"That won't be necessary," he replied in clipped tones. "Bethany won't be participating in drill team."

"Oh? May I ask why?"

"It's too dangerous. She's only eight years old, you know."

"You were eight when you started out in drill team," Shannon pointed out. "So was I, for that matter."

"That was different. You and I were both experienced riders. Bethany isn't."

"Actually, I think she's a very good rider. She has a natural ability. And for the first few practice sessions I'm having them just walk their horses through the movements."

"*I'll* decide what's best for my daughter. I don't want her in drill team."

Bethany had pulled out of the line, and she approached Shannon and her father in time to hear his last words. "Oh, *please,* Daddy," she coaxed, "let me be on the team. Melissa is on it, and we want to do this together. We're best friends.''

Her soft plea smoothed out some of the harsher angles of Clint's face and softened the look in his eyes. It was obvious that it was difficult for him to maintain his stern demeanor where his daughter was concerned. ''You shouldn't have come over here without asking me,'' he scolded gently. ''If Leonard hadn't spotted you heading in this direction on Sandy, I wouldn't even have known where you were.''

''But if I'd asked, you'd have said no,'' the little girl pointed out, with perfect logic.

''That's right, I would have. I don't think you're quite old enough for drill team. Maybe in another year or two. Now you'd better get started home. Thelma is bound to be looking for you. I'll be along in a minute. I need to talk to Shannon.'' He had a few things to say to her about overstepping her area of responsibility.

''But Daddy—''

Clint silenced Bethany with a look that indicated he meant what he said. With an exaggerated sigh, she nudged her horse into a walk and headed toward the exit.

Clint felt a stab of remorse as he watched the small figure. Torn between his reluctance to deny her anything and his desire to protect her from harm, he focused his anger on Shannon. Why did she have to come along and put dangerous ideas into his daughter's head?

But in spite of what he told himself was justifiable indignation, a little twinge of guilt began to nag uncomfortably at him. Although he tried his best to ignore it, it refused to go away until he examined his reasons for being so adamant about not wanting wanting Bethany to be involved in drill team. Could he be at least partly motivated by his wish to avoid any more contact with Shannon than was absolutely necessary?

But that was ridiculous. His only concern was Bethany's safety and well-being. After all, he had every reason to be apprehensive about her riding ability. Having spent the first few years of her life in a city, she wasn't nearly as experienced a rider as most of the drill team members. Here in ranching country most kids were put on a horse almost before they were able to walk, but Bethany hadn't even started learning to ride until they moved back to the ranch when she was four.

That argument wasn't going to work, though. Once he'd started teaching her to ride, she'd taken to it like the proverbial duck to water. Even other people had remarked that she was a natural.

He could see that his nagging conscience wasn't going to give him any peace. With a sigh of resignation, he called, "Just a minute," after Bethany's retreating back. She stopped her horse, but didn't turn around.

He shot a look at Shannon that clearly said, *This is all your fault.* "Maybe we can give it a try," he told the little girl, "if you promise to be very careful."

She wheeled the little bay around and galloped back to her father. Positioning her horse next to his, she leaned out of the saddle and threw her arms around him. "Oh, *thank you,* Daddy!" she cried.

As Shannon caught a glimpse of Clint's face over

Bethany's head, she saw a tenderness revealed there, a gentle softness he usually kept well hidden.

His eyes met hers and the mask slipped back into place. "I'll be dropping by the practice sessions just to keep an eye on things," he said.

Shannon understood that it was a warning—that if any harm befell his daughter, he would hold her personally responsible.

Chapter Four

"Shannon, where do you think we should park the horse trailers?"

"Do you know who brought the box with the hats and flags in it?"

"Which block of stalls is reserved for our horses?"

Shannon found her attention pulled in several directions. As team advisor, she was expected to know all these things. She fielded the questions deftly, doing her best to bring order out of chaos.

In spite of all the confusion, a festive air hung over the show grounds in Fremont, as horses were unloaded from trailers, equipment was stowed away, costumes were unpacked. Tomorrow the team would participate in their first drill competition of the season, and excitement ran high.

The team members, along with parents, chaperones, and assorted townsfolk who had come to act as a cheering section, arrived a day early, to allow time for a few practice sessions in the unfamiliar arena. Shannon had brought a sleeping bag and was planning to sleep outside at the show grounds, along with the members of the team. Some of the adults would be checking into a nearby motel, while those who had campers or motor homes would spend the night at the grounds to help watch over the kids.

More than once during the past three weeks, Shannon had wondered whether the drill team would ever arrive at this point. Oh, it wasn't the kids' fault. She was proud of the way they'd put their all into perfecting the routines. Still, there had been times when she was sorely tempted to resign her temporary post as advisor. She'd made a commitment, though, and she didn't believe in reneging on a promise.

When she'd accepted the position she hadn't counted on Clint showing up at nearly every practice session. She'd tried to ignore his stern presence, to simply go on about the business at hand, but it was unnerving to know he was hovering on the sidelines, his face set into lines of disapproval.

But despite Clint's misgivings and her own dismay over his attitude, the team had pulled itself into shape in a surprisingly short time. Now it was time to find out if all their hard work had paid off. For the kids' sake, she hoped they made a good showing in the ring tomorrow.

Her thoughts were interrupted by a slight tug on her sleeve. She glanced down to see Bethany looking up at her. "What is it, honey?"

"I had to switch saddles—the girth on my old one needs to be replaced—and I'm not sure if the stirrups are the right length. Can you come and see if they need to be shortened?"

"Of course," Shannon replied with a smile, just as if she didn't have a dozen other demands on her time and attention. "I'll be glad to."

Clint, unloading a box of supplies from one of the

equipment trailers, overheard this exchange. Why hadn't Bethany mentioned to him that she needed help? he wondered. "I'll take a look at them—" he began, putting the box down and turning toward his daughter.

But Bethany had already slipped her hand into Shannon's trustingly, and the two were heading off toward the trailer that carried saddles, bridles, and blankets.

He felt a stab of resentment as he watched them walk off together. If Bethany needed something, why hadn't she come to *him* instead of Shannon? She'd always considered him to be all-powerful, and was firmly convinced that he could handle any problem. He'd done his best to not let her down.

Now, all at once, she was turning to someone else. Lately, it was "Shannon this" and "Shannon that," as if her drill team advisor was the last word in wisdom, understanding, and a multitude of other virtues.

There was nothing especially wrong with that, he reminded himself. It was natural for a little girl Bethany's age to develop an affection for someone like Shannon. And he certainly couldn't fault Shannon for the patient attention she was giving the child. Still, he couldn't help wishing his daughter had chosen someone else as a role model.

He told himself jealousy had nothing to do with how he felt. What bothered him was what it might do to Bethany when Shannon returned to Seattle. She'd already had one serious upheaval, when her mother had decided she'd had enough of ranch life. Bethany was better off, of course, without a mother who had cared so little about her that she could walk away with hardly a backward glance. Still, it had been difficult for her. He didn't want her to become too attached to Shannon and then have to adjust to losing her.

Yet, he couldn't very well order her to stay away from Shannon, or ask Shannon to stop being kind to his daughter.

After the horses had been bedded down for the night somebody asked, "Anyone for pizza?"

Several voices eagerly seconded the suggestion. In a matter of minutes a lively group—including Shannon, several other adults, and most of the drill team—was headed for the pizza parlor, a few blocks from the show grounds.

Clint fell into step at the rear where he could keep an unobtrusive eye on Bethany, who was walking arm in arm with her best friend, Melissa. Watching the two little girls, their heads together as they exchanged confidences, he smiled indulgently. He didn't dare get close enough to allow Bethany to see that she was being watched—she was still a little put out over his intention to stay at the show grounds overnight and sleep in the covered bed of his pickup truck.

"Daddy," she'd moaned, rolling her eyes heavenward, with the air of one who was sorely put upon.

Eight, going on twenty-seven, Clint thought ruefully. Maybe he *was* being overprotective, but—doggone it—wasn't it a father's duty to keep his daughter safe from harm?

He had to admit this drill team thing was working out better than he'd expected it to. Bethany took her position on the team seriously, and was developing a real sense of responsibility about such matters as memorizing the routines, getting to practice on time, and keeping her horse groomed. There was no doubt about it, Shannon was a good influence on his daughter.

He felt a pang of guilt as he recalled how he'd made life miserable for Shannon by hanging around disapprovingly during her practice sessions, as if he expected something terrible to happen. He'd obviously underestimated her ability to keep her young charges in hand. She didn't allow horseplay or rowdiness among the team members, and the kids all seemed to respect her quiet authority.

His conscience told him he owed her an apology. Surprisingly, he didn't find the prospect nearly as daunting as he'd expected to. In fact, he felt a sense of relief, as if a weight had been lifted from him. Once he'd admitted to himself that she had only the best interests of Bethany, as well as the other team members, at heart, it had been difficult trying to maintain his initial disapproval. He hadn't known exactly how to make amends, but now he decided his best course of action would be the direct approach.

He scanned the group for a glimpse of her. When he spotted her she was waving a greeting to someone, and her upraised arm emphasized the graceful lines of her slender body. Something constricted in his throat as his glance lingered admiringly on the attractive picture she made. She was utterly unconscious of the effect she was creating as she leaned down to make a laughing comment to one of the kids, her thick auburn hair falling to one side of her face like a lustrous curtain.

Quickening his pace, he started to make his way

through the crowd toward her, then slowed down, a muttered exclamation on his lips . . .

As Shannon strolled along, enjoying the warm summer evening and the lighthearted camaradarie, she became aware that a tall, lean figure had fallen into step beside her. *Clint!* She'd spotted him bringing up the rear when they started out. Her nerves tingled with awareness, until she glanced up and saw that it wasn't Clint, it was Tim Elliot, a former classmate, and now a history teacher at the high school they'd both attended. She smiled up at him, suppressing her pang of disappointment. It wasn't *his* fault he wasn't Clint. He was a good friend and she was genuinely pleased to see him.

"I thought that was you," he said, matching his step to hers. "I heard you were the team advisor now."

"Just until they find someone to take over permanently. I didn't expect to see you here."

"A couple of my students are on the team, so I promised them I'd come along to cheer them on."

"Great. We need all the support we can get."

They made light, easy talk as they strolled along, about old times and old friends. When they reached the pizza parlor they slid into adjacent seats at the long rustic table, still deep in conversation. Shannon couldn't help noticing that Clint was seated at the other end of the table.

After a brief interruption while they ordered their pizza, Tim continued bringing her up-to-date on several mutual acquaintances. When that subject was exhausted, the discussion turned to shared experiences from their high school days.

Several times Shannon's laughter rang out as amusing events came to mind. "Remember when Chuck Willis got on the PA system and announced that classes were being canceled for the day because the plumbing was out of order?"

"Yeah," Tim replied in an envious tone. "I was jealous because I hadn't thought of it. Some of the kids were already out the door by the time Mr. Stinson got wind of what was happening."

"As I recall, you had your moments," Shannon reminded him. "How about that time you initiated a hunger strike in the cafeteria because the cook served liver for the third time that month."

"Shh," Tim cautioned, glancing around guiltily. "Now that I've defected to the 'other side,' I have to be careful of my image. If my students ever learned about some of the things I did, I'd completely lose my credibility." Lowering his voice, he tilted his head close to Shannon's confidentially, so they could continue their reminiscing without being overheard.

Shannon's attention was diverted briefly when several large pizzas were brought to the table. She glanced up, pausing in the middle of what she was saying to Tim. The rest of the sentence died on her lips, as her gaze met Clint's.

Something flickered in Clint's dark eyes, something that reached out and drew her to him, rendering her powerless to look away. For a moment hardly longer than a heartbeat, Shannon and Clint were completely alone, the only two people in the world. Everything around them blurred into nothingness, the laughter and chatter of their companions, the yeasty, spicy aroma of pizza, the nasal twang emanating from the jukebox as a singer lamented his lost love.

Vaguely, she became aware that Tim was saying something to her. All at once the spell was broken. "Wh-what?" she murmured, making an attempt to pull her attention back to her surroundings.

"I just asked if you wanted pepperoni or Canadian bacon."

"Oh. Ah, either one."

She accepted the slice of pizza Tim held out to her and bit into it automatically, but her appetite had left her. She might as well have been munching a piece of cardboard, for all the taste it had. As she ate she was aware of Clint's eyes on her, watching her every move.

It was a relief when the get-together at the pizza parlor began to break up.

When the group returned to the show grounds everyone gathered inside the large circle made by the campers and horse trailers. The glow of flashlights and lanterns in the darkness, and the country-western music pouring out of a portable boom box, added to the holiday mood.

After a while Shannon noticed some of the younger kids beginning to yawn. "I think it's about time to call it a night," she announced. "Tomorrow's a big day."

There was a chorus of protests, but she was firm, and eventually all the team members were settled into sleeping bags, girls on one side of the clearing and boys on the other.

The grown-ups gradually drifted away, to go into

their campers or head back to the motel, and after a lot of whispering and muffled giggles, Shannon's young charges quieted down at last. Shannon herself was wide awake, though, a multitude of thoughts running through her mind. Part of her jitteriness was due to simple stage fright. As team advisor, she was understandably anxious for them to do well tomorrow, in their first official public appearance of the season. Although she wouldn't be in the ring with them, she would be going through every single maneuver with them in spirit.

Her attack of nerves wasn't due entirely to anticipation over the coming competition, though. She was acutely aware of Clint's presence, just on the other side of the clearing. Her thoughts went back to those few moments in the pizza parlor when he had let down his guard briefly. For just a second she'd almost thought he was beginning to have some feelings for her, but she told herself she was imagining things. Most likely, the only reason he'd been watching her so closely was because he felt she should be paying more attention to the kids on the team, and less to Tim.

She sat on the grass for a long time, arms wrapped around her knees, gazing up at the stars. Finally, too keyed up to sleep, she decided to go for a walk. She wasn't sure where she was headed as she made her way across the grounds in the darkness. She wandered through the barn, making a casual check of the horses in their stalls, then found herself at the arena, staring out into the deserted show ring.

"I see you couldn't sleep either." Clint's deep voice at her elbow took her by surprise. "I was feeling a little restless, so I thought maybe some exercise would help.''

Shannon bit back an exclamation of dismay. Right now Clint was the last person she wanted to be around. After all, wasn't he the reason she hadn't been able to settle down? ''I just thought I should look in on the horses one last time,'' she explained, hoping he'd continue on his way.

He made no move to leave, though. Without turning her head, Shannon cast a sidelong glance at him. He was resting his arms on the top rail of the fence, not looking at her.

After several seconds of silence, he said, ''I owe you an apology.''

The words seemed to hang there in the still night air. Was this some kind of trick? Shannon wondered. ''Oh?'' she responded, keeping her voice expressionless.

He turned to face her. ''I'm sorry I gave you such a hard time about the drill team. Being on the team has been good for Bethany. Truce?''

Shannon was caught off guard by his offer. Did he think after the way he had behaved all he had to do was say ''I'm sorry,'' and all would be forgiven? The memory of the way he'd stormed into the arena, that first day of drill practice, still evoked a flash of resentment in her. Her initial impulse was to let him know, in no uncertain terms, that she hadn't forgotten his overbearing attitude. She found herself unable to deliver the scathing reply that sprang to her lips, though. She sensed what it had cost him to swallow his pride and admit he had been wrong.

"Truce," she agreed, accepting the hand he extended in a conciliatory gesture.

As his fingers closed around hers, the brief contact sent a tingle all the way up her arm. Fortunately, he didn't seem to have heard her sudden, involuntary intake of breath. She managed to extricate her hand from his before he had a chance to notice the effect his touch had on her.

Clint shifted nervously from one foot to the other. Shannon had the feeling there was more he wanted to say.

"I, ah, I've been meaning to tell you how much I appreciate the attention you've been giving Bethany," he went on. "She thinks the world of you, you know. She talks about you all the time."

"I enjoy doing things for Bethany," Shannon replied. "She's a sweet child, and I'm very fond of her."

"She's the most important thing in my life."

The simple statement tugged at Shannon's heart. Perhaps she hadn't been quite as sympathetic as she could have been when he'd objected to Bethany's being in drill team. Granted, he might have displayed a little more tact, but he was, after all, just a father who was concerned about his child's well-being.

"It must be difficult raising a daughter by yourself." As soon as the words were out, Shannon wished she could take them back. He might resent being reminded of his failed marriage.

But he didn't seem to have taken offense. "It *is* hard sometimes, trying to be both father and mother. Thelma does the best she can, of course, but . . ."

His voice trailed off, as if he realized he'd let down

his guard more than he'd intended to. He took his hat off and ran a hand through his hair in a gesture that seemed to indicate his helplessless. The movement made Shannon want to reach out and comfort him.

She managed to catch herself before she did anything she knew she'd regret later. ''I-I'd better get back now,'' she stammered.

She made no move to leave, though. Her limbs had lost their ability to do her bidding. Hesitantly, she glanced up at him. For just a second she saw something in his eyes . . .

It was gone so quickly, though, she decided it must have been a trick of the shifting nighttime shadows. She took a step backward so she could look look into his face, and almost lost her balance. He put his hands on her shoulders to steady her.

His expression, in the moonlight, was unreadable, but all at once Shannon was aware of his nearness, of the aura of masculinity that emanated from him. Her heart seemed to be beating more rapidly than usual, and disturbing thoughts began to take control of her consciousness—thoughts about how it would feel to be held in those strong arms and pressed against that lean, muscular body. For just a few seconds she felt utterly powerless to resist the subtle electricity that had suddenly sprung up between them.

The mood was broken as a nervous whinny came from the stable.

''I have to see if the horses are all right,'' she murmured, deftly shrugging free of his grasp and hurrying toward the horse barn.

*   *   *

The next morning Shannon managed to avoid Clint as much as possible. That wasn't too difficult, with so much to be done. The team practiced in the ring, with Shannon keeping a sharp eye out for even the slightest imperfection in their routine. Then the horses were groomed until every hair was in place, and the tack and costumes brought out and examined for any last-minute repairs.

At last the start of the competition was announced. The riders waited, costumed and ready, outside the arena, critically watching the teams that performed ahead of them. Shannon gave them a few final instructions as she went down the line, nervously adjusting hats, neckerchiefs, and bridles.

When the announcer's voice came over the loud-speaker, ". . . Silver Spurs drill team, from the town of Liberty . . ." twenty-four young riders straightened in their saddles and gathered up twenty-four pairs of reins.

Instead of going up into the stands Shannon remained where she was, near the entrance to the area, along with several of the parents and other spectators. From her vantage point, she watched the team gallop into the ring. Identically attired in black pants and boots, turquoise shirts, white vests, hats, and neckerchiefs, and spotless white gloves, each rider carrying a flag, they made an impressive spectacle. The bright costumes and stirring march music, the horses' flying manes and tails, and the colorful flags rippling in the breeze all combined into a symphony of sights and sounds.

As the riders went through their routine, she found herself giving instructions under her breath. ''Don't get too close to the horse in front . . . keep your backs straight . . . don't let that flag droop . . .''

She couldn't help tensing up when they reached the point in the drill where two lines of riders intersected in the middle of the ring, as the entire team formed a continuous moving figure eight. Each rider had to adjust his horse's gait to avoid colliding with the horse approaching from the opposite direction, and the slightest miscalculation could throw the entire team out of step. She let her breath out slowly as the last person in line completed the maneuver and Matt led the group into the next movement.

The hours of practice were paying off, and the entire team moved in perfect unison, as if controlled by a single mind. When they finished their routine, there was an excitement in the air that could almost be touched and tasted. There was still one last team that had to perform before the judges could make their decision. The riders, still on horseback, waited outside the arena.

And then the announcer was saying, ''. . . first place, Silver Spurs drill team . . .''

Shannon could hardly believe what she was hearing. They'd done it. They'd actually taken first place! A jubilant cheer went up when the team rode triumphantly into the ring to receive their award. In a spontaneous burst of joy, Shannon turned and bestowed an enthusiastic hug on the person nearest her.

Her elation quickly turned to dismay as she realized Clint was the recipient of her exuberant embrace. ''I— ah, I'm sorry,'' she stammered, struggling to regain her composure. ''I-I just—''

Before she could back away his own arms came

around her, hesitantly at first. Then they tightened, and Shannon's limbs suddenly felt weak, as if they were melting. She was barely aware of the applause from the crowd, the announcer's voice congratulating the team, the sound of horses' hooves. At this moment nothing mattered except the incredible sweetness of being held in Clint's embrace. Her cheek rested against his chest, and she could hear his heart beating next to her ear.

This would never do, she told herself, forcing her tangled emotions back into order. She glanced up, intending to make some kind of lighthearted remark about letting her enthusiasm get the better of her. But the words died away as her eyes met Clint's. His lips were just inches from hers. A slight movement was all it would take . . .

She was brought back to sanity by the sound of approaching hoofbeats. Glancing around, she saw that they were surrounded by the entire drill team.

"We—we were just congratulating each other," she murmured, twisting out of Clint's embrace. Did he seem reluctant to release her?

The riders glanced at one another and grinned.

"You kids looked really good out there," she said in a brisk tone. "Now then, let's have a look at that trophy." When Matt handed it over she avoided looking at Clint as she inspected it closely.

Out of the corner of her eye she noticed the way Bethany's eyes widened with delight, as a secret look passed between her and Melissa.

Chapter Five

Standing in front of the hall mirror, John scowled at his reflection. "Maureen, where are you?" he thundered. "I need you to tie this thing for me. I can't get it right." He yanked the offending strip of cloth from around his neck and glared at it.

"Goodness, don't get in such an uproar," his wife scolded gently as she came to his aid. She was wearing a black dinner dress, partially zipped up the back. "You'd think anyone who can wrestle down and brand a calf could manage a little thing like a necktie." Deftly, she tied it for him and slid the knot up. "There," she said, patting it into place and standing back to survey her handiwork. "You look very handsome."

"I don't see why I have to get all duded up for this thing, anyway," he growled.

"Now, John," Maureen said in a soothing tone, "it won't hurt you to put on a suit and tie for the occasion. It's only once a year."

Shannon couldn't help smiling as she listened to this exchange between her parents. Her father had been grumbling all day about having to dress up for the annual Ranchers' Association dinner. Like most of his contemporaries, he'd almost rather be dragged by wild horses than have to wear something other than his usual denim jeans and western shirt.

As John stalked off down the hall, his cast making a heavy, thumping sound, Maureen turned her back to Shannon. "Zip me up, will you?"

"I thought Dad would have calmed down a little, now that he's out of his wheelchair and can get around on his own," Shannon commented as she manipulated the zipper.

"I try not to take it personally when he gets like this," Maureen replied, smoothing the dress down over a figure that the years of helping with ranch chores had kept as slim as her daughter's. "He doesn't mean to be such a grouch. It's just that once he got out of the wheelchair he expected to be able to do everything he'd done before the accident—"

She broke off what she was saying to answer a knock at the door. "Oh, hello, Sam," she greeted the foreman. "Come in."

"Evening, ma'am. Your husband around?"

"Right here." John limped into the room. "What's up?"

"It's Bess. I think she's about ready. Thought you'd want to know."

John nodded. "I figured she'd foal any day now. How's she doing?"

"Not too well," Sam replied. "It looks like she might be in for a rough time."

"Hmm. I'd better go have a look."

"You can't go out to the barn in your good clothes," Maureen protested, but almost before she had the words out John was following Sam out the door.

"Sometimes I get the feeling he thinks more of that mare than he does of me," she remarked wryly.

"You'd better go on to the dinner without me," John said to his wife when he returned a few minutes later. "I can't leave Bess while she needs me. As soon as I get out of this monkey suit I'm going back out to the barn."

"This is ridiculous," Maureen argued. "It isn't as if this was Bess's first foal. She'll manage just fine without any help from you. Sam will be there if she needs—"

But John was already on his way upstairs to change. Helplessly, Maureen watched the retreating form. With an expression of resignation, she turned to her daughter. "I should have known he'd find some way to get out of going. I guess I might as well get into something comfortable."

"You mean you're not going if Dad doesn't go?"

Maureen shook her head. "I'd better stay here and keep an eye on him. If I don't, he'll be out in the barn all night with that mare. It hasn't been that long since his accident, and he can't seem to get it through his head that he still has to take things easy. Tell you what," she said, as if an idea had just come to her, "*you* can go to the dinner. That way at least one of the tickets won't go to waste."

"Oh, no, I'd feel out of place going alone," Shannon protested.

"I don't see why. Just about everybody there will be people you've known all your life."

"I didn't bring a dinner dress."

But Maureen was not to be deterred. "That's no

problem. You can wear something of mine," she said, as if that settled the matter.

"I can't wear your clothes. You know I'm a good two inches taller than you."

Maureen dismissed this last objection with an airy wave of her hand. "All the better to show off those long slim legs of yours."

Knowing how determined her mother could be once she'd made up her mind about something, Shannon decided there was little point in arguing. She allowed herself to be whisked upstairs, where she slipped out of the terry-cloth robe she'd donned after her shower, and put on the slip and panty hose Maureen supplied. A few minutes later she was being zipped into a blue dress in a soft, clingy fabric.

"It certainly looks better on you than it ever did on me," Maureen remarked, standing back to take an appraising look. "Try these with it." She handed her daughter a pair of gold earrings, set with sparkly stones, and a pendant to match. "Now let's see what we can do about your hair." In a few deft motions, she twisted Shannon's thick hair up onto her head and secured it with glittery clips, leaving a few stray tendrils to curl around her face and at the nape of her neck.

"Am I supposed to go to the dinner barefoot?" Shannon asked, wiggling her nylon-clad toes. "Or maybe in my boots?"

"Oh. Just a minute. Now where are they—" Maureen's words were muffled as she rummaged in her closet. "Aha!" she exclaimed triumphantly, emerging with a pair of high-heeled sandals the same color as the dress.

As Shannon stepped into the shoes she surveyed her reflection in the full-length mirror. She had to admit the total effect *was* rather attractive. Since coming back home she'd practically lived in jeans, so it was kind of fun to have an opportunity to dress up. And it *would* be enjoyable to see people she hadn't seen in years. She realized she was glad her mother had talked her into going.

"Where are the keys to the pickup?" she asked as she came downstairs.

"Oh, you won't need—" Maureen's words were interrupted by a knock at the door.

It was probably Sam with some word from her father, Shannon thought as she went to answer it. Pulling the door open, she started to ask, "How's Bess—" but the words died on her lips when she found herself looking at Clint.

By now she had been home long enough that she wasn't completely undone by every chance encounter with him. Still, she was unprepared for the sight of him on her doorstep, looking so alarmingly attractive that she felt an odd little flutter in the pit of her stomach. The western-cut suit he was wearing set off his trim, lean-hipped build to perfection, and the white dress shirt emphasized his deep, even tan. A faint aroma of some tangy after-shave teased her senses. All at once her knees felt weak and her insides seems to be turning to jelly. The thought, *I wonder if I'm coming down with something,* crossed her mind.

For just a second she thought she caught a glimmer of admiration in Clint's eyes. It was gone so soon she might have imagined it, though, and was replaced by something that looked like surprise or confusion. What was *he* doing here? she wondered.

"Oh, I see your ride is here," Maureen commented to Shannon, coming up behind here. "Come in, Clint."

Automatically, Shannon stepped aside to allow Clint to enter. Her *ride?* What was her mother talking about?

"There's been a slight change in plans," Maureen said to Clint. Briefly, she explained how her husband had insisted on staying home to keep an eye on the mare. "Of course, that means I have to stay home too, to see that he doesn't overdo it," she went on.

"Bess is foaling?" There was a note of interest in Clint's voice. "I'd better see if I can help." He turned and would have gone out the door, but Maureen deftly intercepted him.

"Sam is out there with him," she said, with her hand on the doorknob. "Between the two of them, I'm sure Bess has more help than she needs. Besides, Shannon is going to the dinner, so your trip over here wasn't wasted."

Seeing her daughter's bewildered expression, Maureen turned to her. "Didn't I mention, dear, that Clint had offered to come by and pick us up so we could all go to the dinner together?"

"No, I don't think you did," Shannon murmured, struggling to hide her dismay at this unexpected development. Turning to Clint, she said, "That was very kind of you, but I can drive myself. I'm sorry you made the trip over here for nothing."

"Nonsense," Maureen put in. "As long as Clint is

already here, and you're both headed for the same place, it would be foolish to take two vehicles.''

Clint had been silent during this exchange. Ever since the door had opened, the sight of Shannon in that figure-hugging blue dress had rendered him all but incapable of rational speech. His mouth felt dry and he seemed to be having trouble drawing a deep breath.

He hadn't wanted to go to this dinner. He much preferred to spend his evenings at home with Bethany, or puttering around the ranch. This was sort of an obligatory thing, though. As a board member, he was expected to attend. He tried to concentrate on what Maureen was saying—something about Shannon riding to the dinner with him.

Shannon stole a glance at Clint, but it was impossible to tell how he felt about this turn of events. His features revealed nothing of what he was thinking. Just because they'd declared a truce, that didn't mean he wanted her company for an entire evening. ''I wouldn't dream of imposing on you,'' she said, keeping her tone politely impersonal. ''I might decide to come home early, and I wouldn't want you to have to leave in the middle of things.''

Clint made a valiant effort to pull himself together. ''That won't be a problem. I'll be glad to have a good excuse to get away early. Some of those after-dinner speakers can get a little long-winded.''

''There, that settles it,'' Maureen said briskly. ''You two run along and have a good time.''

With a sinking feeling, Shannon decided it was probably easier to give in than to make an issue of the matter. After all, she couldn't come up with any valid reason for not accepting the ride that was being offered, and if she protested too much, it might appear that she was *afraid* to be alone with Clint.

How did I get myself into a situation like this? she wondered, as her mother held the door open for them. Hadn't she already made a big enough mess of things? Ever since she'd come home she'd done her best to maintain a cool, detached attitude around Clint, and then she'd ruined everything by throwing herself into his arms last week at the drill competition. She still could hardly believe she'd done that. It had been purely a reflex action, of course. She'd been so delighted over the team taking first place that she hadn't been able to resist the urge to hug someone. Unfortunately, that "someone" had been Clint, simply because he'd happened to be the nearest person.

If she had to lose control that way, she fervently wished it hadn't been in front of the entire drill team and a good portion of the local citizenry. News traveled fast in a small town like Liberty, and by now the good people of the town had probably blown the incident all out of proportion. And showing up at the Ranchers' Association dinner with Clint certainly wouldn't help matters any.

Besides, now that she'd discovered she couldn't trust herself to behave in a rational manner where Clint was concerned, she was going to have to be on her guard every second, to avoid doing anything foolish.

Once they were in Clint's pickup truck, Shannon's discomfort increased. Although the cab of the truck was roomy enough to accommodate three people comfortably, it seemed small and crowded. The aura of virility Clint exuded was almost a tangible substance, filling the enclosed area. All the emotions she had struggled to put out of her mind came flooding back, threatening to overwhelm her.

She had to get herself under control and maintain some semblance of normal behavior before Clint sensed what his closeness was doing to her. It would help break the tension if they could make casual conversation, but it appeared they were destined to ride all the way into town in total silence. She couldn't think of a thing to say that didn't sound utterly inane. She drew a deep breath, fighting down a wave of panic.

She froze as he glanced over at her, a questioning expression on his face. Surely if he looked into her eyes he'd be able to see what she'd tried so hard to keep hidden from him. To avoid making eye contact she focused her gaze on the thin white scar at one corner of his mouth. Although it had faded considerably over the years, the memory of how he had received it was as vivid as the day it had happened. . . .

He'd been in his teens at the time and had accepted a challenge from a couple of his friends to ride one of his father's unbroken horses.

Peering wide-eyed around a corner of the barn, Shannon had grasped, even at ten years of age, that it was only through sheer determination that he was able to stay on for the agreed-upon length of time. As soon as the time limit was up and he relaxed slightly, a triumphant grin on his face, the bucking animal sent him sailing over the corral fence.

Shannon still recalled how her heart had leapt into her throat at the sight of him lying pale and still on the ground, a slight trickle of blood coming from the small cut near his mouth. She'd been almost limp with relief when his eyelids fluttered open and he managed a shaky version of his usual happy-go-lucky smile.

She also recalled how the discomfort from his cuts and bruises had seemed to pale in comparison to the elder Gallagher's considerable wrath on learning of his son's foolhardy stunt. Clint had accepted his father's tongue-lashing stoically, however, as if he considered it a fair price to pay for those few moments of daredevil recklessness. . . .

She couldn't imagine this silent, distant stranger throwing caution to the winds that way and doing something brash and impetuous, just for the fun of it.

As Clint maneuvered the truck onto the highway, he was acutely aware of Shannon seated next to him. Just the thought of the way she looked in that silky blue dress was so distracting that he was having trouble keeping his mind on his driving. He couldn't help recalling how she'd felt in his arms when she'd hugged him at the drill competition. . . .

With a jerky motion he yanked the steering wheel to the left, as the vehicle started to veer toward the shoulder of the road. "Oops, sorry," he muttered. *Pay attention,* he told himself. If he wasn't careful he was going to land both of them in the ditch, and *that* would put the crowning touch to an evening that had already gotten off to a less-than-promising start. He realized he could have shown a little more enthusiasm when he'd found out Shannon was riding to the dinner with him, but this whole thing had caught him off guard. He'd expected to spend an uneventful few hours in the company of her parents.

He looked over at her out of the corner of his eye,

but she was staring straight ahead. It occurred to him that she probably wasn't enjoying this any more than he was. Riding along this way, neither of them saying a word, was getting to be doggone uncomfortable.

He reminded himself that they were both mature people. They'd been thrown together for the evening, like it or not, so he supposed they might as well make the best of it. They ought to be able to at least make small talk rather than each of them trying to pretend the other didn't exist.

He cast about in his mind for some reasonably safe topic, and came up with the only subject he could think of that might be a common ground for normal conversation.

"The drill team made a pretty good showing last week, didn't they?" he ventured.

His mention of the drill team reminded Shannon once again of her impulsive behavior the day of the competition. She was thankful for the darkness so he couldn't see how her cheeks were flaming. "Yes, they did," she replied cautiously. "I was very proud of them."

"You deserve all the credit, you know," Clint continued, somewhat encouraged. "You've done a great job with those kids."

"I'm glad I was asked to be their advisor. I've enjoyed every minute of it." Well, maybe not every minute, she amended mentally, recalling how difficult Clint had made things for her. But he *had* apologized. "Working with the team has given me a chance to feel I'm part of the community again, instead of just someone passing through. Liberty *is* my home, you know, and I've really missed it."

He gave her a curious glance. "You've been away—how long?"

Was there a faintly accusatory tone to his question, as if to remind her that it had been her choice to stay away, or was she reading too much into an innocent remark? "Except for a few quick trips home to see the folks, it's been eight years," she replied, "counting the four years I was away at college."

"What made you decide to move to Seattle after college, instead of coming back here?"

"Oh, lots of things—better job opportunities . . ." Her voice trailed off vaguely. She couldn't let him know that *he* was the reason she hadn't come back.

"I suppose you're anxious to return to Seattle. You probably find things a little slow around here after life in the city."

Suppressing a stab of resentment, Shannon reminded herself he was only making conversation. She had to stop finding these hidden meanings in everything he said. "Actually, I'm thoroughly enjoying my stay here. If nothing else good came of Dad's accident, at least it gave me a reason to have a good, long visit at home."

"I suppose your boss will be glad to have you back."

Now what was *that* supposed to mean? she wondered. She recalled his stony expression that time he'd been more or less forced into delivering the roses Paul had sent. Did he think there was something going on between her and Paul? And even if there had been, what business was it of his?

More than likely, though, he was simply trying to find out how soon her job responsibilities would take her back to Seattle. Was he really so anxious to be rid of her? she wondered with a little pang.

It occurred to her once again that maybe the memory of the way she'd once thrown herself at him was making him uncomfortable. Well, if that was what was worrying him, he could rest easy, she thought. She vowed that nothing would make her reveal how she felt about him.

"I'm sure Paul misses my *work,*" she said coolly. "I've put a lot of time and effort into helping him get his business started."

"I'll bet," Clint muttered under his breath.

Shannon gave him a curious look. "What was that?"

"Nothing. I was just talking to myself." *That was a close one,* he thought. True, the idea of Shannon spending a lot of time helping this guy get his business started evoked a mental picture of the two of them working late together, in a deserted office . . .

Determinedly, he put the disturbing image out of his mind. If he wasn't careful Shannon was going to suspect what the thought of her with this . . . this *Paul* guy did to him. Maybe he'd be better off to just keep still, since trying to make conversation was like navigating a mine field.

They rode the rest of the way into town in silence. It was a relief when the restaurant came into view.

Chapter Six

By the time Clint maneuvered the pickup into the parking lot, his conscience was beginning to nag at him. If the ride into town had been uncomfortable, he was as much to blame as Shannon. More so, actually. It wasn't her fault that the sight of her in that clingy blue dress set all his senses on fire. Or that he went a little crazy thinking about her with that guy in Seattle.

It's time you got your act together, Gallagher, he told himself sternly. Shannon wouldn't be here much longer, and it wouldn't hurt him to at least behave with common courtesy instead of acting like some spoiled kid.

With that thought in mind, he got out of the truck and hurried around to open Shannon's door. "Shall we?" he said.

She looked surprised, and for a moment he was afraid she was going to ignore the arm he held out to her. After a few seconds, though, she accepted it and allowed him to assist her in getting out of the truck.

As Shannon and Clint approached the banquet room they could hear the muted hum of voices, the clink of ice cubes in glasses, and an occasional burst of laughter. It sounded as if the pre-dinner social hour was in full swing.

Shannon was sure this whole thing must be as much a strain on Clint as it was on her, but at least they'd be able to relax once they were inside. Now that Clint had fulfilled his obligation to deliver her to the dinner, he wouldn't feel compelled to stay by her side all evening. They'd both be able to circulate and talk to other people, and she would be free of the necessity of guarding every word and gesture.

But the minute she and Clint walked through the wide double doors into the banquet room, she sensed a subtle change in the atmosphere around them. Several conversations broke off in mid-sentence. Those who had spotted them first nudged others, and a little unseen current went around the room as heads turned and speculative glances were exchanged.

Puzzled, Shannon looked down at herself to see if her slip was showing or her shoes didn't match. "What's wrong?" she whispered to Clint. "Why is everyone staring at us?" But before he could reply, a plump, middle-aged matron bore down on them.

"My, it certainly is a treat to see the two of you here together," Harriet Polk gushed. "When I saw you come in I told Roy, 'If I ever saw two people who belong together, it's Clint Gallagher and Shannon McCrae,' Didn't I, Roy?" She turned to the mild-appearing man in her wake for verification.

"Yep, that's exactly what she said," Roy Polk confirmed. His tone indicated that he had long since given up trying to stem his wife's runaway enthusiasms.

The dry amusement in his manner was lost on Harriet, who continued, "I've known both of you since you were babies, and I've *always* felt you were destined for each other. And then when I heard how—

well, how *close* you were at the drill competition, I knew I'd been right all along.''

''Oh, but we're not—'' Shannon began.

''Winnie, come over here.'' Harriet reached out to detain another woman who was walking past. ''I just want you to see this. Don't they make a nice-looking couple?''

Shannon glanced up at Clint and saw that he was just as stunned over this turn of events as she was. As Winnie looked them up and down, they submitted self-consciously to her scrutiny.

''No doubt about it, they're the best-looking couple here,'' Winnie agreed, giving them a nod of approval.

Shannon stood rooted to the spot, in an agony of embarrassment. This couldn't be happening! She had to get things straightened out before the good ladies of Liberty had them married and setting up house-keeping. She tried again. ''We, ah, we just—''

''It's about time you two saw the light,'' Harriet said. She turned to Winnie. ''Remember how cute they were when they were children, with Shannon always following Clint around, and him being so patient with her?''

It was obvious nothing Shannon could say was going to get through to the two women. They weren't going to be deterred by anything as mundane as *facts*. She realized this must be every bit as uncomfortable for Clint as it was for her. In some vague way, she felt responsible. After all, it hadn't been *his* idea for her to accompany him tonight. ''I'm sorry I got you into this,'' she said under her breath.

In reply, he gave an offhanded shrug. Shannon had

no idea whether it meant *It's not your fault,* or *It doesn't matter,* or something else.

But it *did* matter, and it *was* her fault. If she'd stood her ground when her mother had insisted she come to this dinner . . .

It was too late, though, to start lamenting about what she *should* have done. "What are we going to do?" she asked helplessly. "We can't let them think—"

"It doesn't look like there's much we *can* do. Nothing we say will convince them they've jumped to a wrong conclusion."

A quick glance at the two women, who had their heads together in a conspiratorial way, confirmed Clint's words.

They're probably naming our firstborn, Shannon thought with dismay.

"Look, there are the Hicksons," Clint said to Shannon, pointing out a couple across the room. "I know you'll want to go over and say hello to them." He turned to Harriet and Winnie with a polite smile. "Will you excuse us? There are so many people here that Shannon hasn't seen since she's been back . . ." With this, he linked his arm through Shannon's and drew her away.

Thank goodness, Shannon thought. At least Clint had had the presence of mind to get them out of a touchy situation, while she, on the other hand, had just stood there like a ninny, unable to do anything except stutter and stammer.

Now that they were away from the two matchmakers, she just might survive the rest of the evening without dying of embarrassment. Surely the other guests wouldn't be so quick to pair them off.

But that hope was dashed when they approached the little knot of people on the other side of the room, and were greeted with knowing looks and benevolent smiles.

Although Shannon had had every intention of going off on her own once she and Clint arrived at the restaurant, she found her plans thwarted at every turn. There seemed to be a conspiracy by the other guests to keep them together. Every time she attempted to leave his side she found her way unobtrusively blocked. Or she was drawn back into the conversation in such a way that she couldn't leave without appearing rude.

Apparently it was true that "all the world loves a lover." She felt as if they were on display. Everyone seemed to have concluded that they were an item, and they were all obviously delighted.

There didn't seem to be much she could do about it, short of marching up to the microphone on the speakers' platform and announcing to the entire local chapter of the Ranchers' Association that she and Clint were *not* romantically involved.

Her only other option was to simply go along with it, to smile noncommittally and take the teasing remarks and the veiled—and not-so-veiled—hints in stride. It would be embarrassing, of course, but it was only for one evening. She really didn't have much choice anyway. There was no way she was going to convince all these people there was absolutely *nothing* between her and Clint—especially after her little display at the drill competition.

By the time dinner was served she felt as if her facial muscles were frozen into a permanent smile. She wondered how Clint was taking this. To his credit, he seemed to be handling the situation fairly well, although, as usual, it was awfully hard to tell what he was thinking. Did he resent being put in such a position?

It was a relief when the meal was over and the committee chairmen began giving their annual reports. At least now she and Clint were spared having to contend with all those leading remarks about wedding bells, Shannon thought.

Although she tried to listen attentively to the committee reports, she couldn't stifle a yawn when one of the chairmen droned on for what seemed an interminable time. Glancing up, she saw that Clint was watching her. His lips twitched slightly, as if he were amused.

"What do you say we make our break as soon as this guy finishes talking?" he said in a low voice, leaning close to her. "We can leave before the next speaker gets started."

"We can't just get up and walk out, with everybody watching us," she whispered back. "What would people think?"

He considered this for a moment. "Tell you what. Why don't you pretend to be heading for the ladies' room, and I'll start edging toward the door? They'll just assume I'm going out for a cigarette or something."

"But you don't smoke."

"I'd be willing to take it up if it'll get us out of

here. I don't think I can sit through another of those long-winded committee reports.''

Shannon was so grateful to him for coming up with a way for them to make a graceful exit that she could have hugged him! She caught herself just in time, though. *Yeah, great idea,* she thought wryly, choking back a giggle just before it reached her lips. Wasn't that what had gotten her into trouble in the first place? If she hadn't thoughtlessly thrown her arms around him in a sudden burst of unrestrained enthusiasm, maybe other people wouldn't be so eager to pair them off.

Lowering her gaze demurely in case anyone happened to be looking their way, she signaled her agreement with a barely perceptible nod. When she raised her eyes she saw Harriet Polk beaming at her and Clint approvingly. *She probably thinks he was whispering 'sweet nothings' to me,* Shannon thought, feeling a blush stain her cheeks.

When the speaker finally wound down, Shannon murmured a brief ''Excuse me,'' and, striving for a casual air, sauntered out into the hall, where Clint joined her a few minutes later.

''Let's get going before our fan club discovers we've made our break,'' he said, putting a hand on her shoulder and steering her toward the exit.

''I feel like a criminal,'' Shannon commented as they made their way through the parking lot. ''Ouch!''

''Are you all right?'' Clint asked, a note of concern in his voice.

''I just stubbed my toe on a rock. Open-toed, high-heeled sandals aren't exactly the thing for walking through gravel. And I can't see a thing out here.''

"We're almost there. The truck is right over here. Take my hand." He reached out and grasped her small hand in his large one.

Shannon tried to ignore the pleasant tingle generated by the light contact, concentrating instead on finding her way in the darkness. "I can't believe we really did that," she said when they were finally in the pickup truck, heading out toward the highway. "Wouldn't it have been easier to just say good-bye, and tell people we were leaving?"

"Then we'd have really gotten some raised eyebrows. They'd have thought we couldn't wait to be alone."

"They'll think that anyway," she pointed out.

"But at least we won't be there to see it. I don't know if I could have handled any more of those knowing looks or sly winks."

Had he minded that much? Shannon wondered, studying his profile in the darkness. His expression revealed nothing.

"Look, I really am sorry I got you into this." She repeated her earlier apology.

"Hey, don't blame yourself because everyone got the wrong idea. It wasn't anybody's fault. And we did serve a useful purpose."

"We *did?*" What in the world was that supposed to mean?

"Well, sometimes these Ranchers' Association dinners can be deadly boring. At least we livened up the evening for the other guests."

Shannon shot him a look. Although his tone was perfectly serious, she detected a hint of a twinkle in his eye.

"It was nice of us to provide entertainment," Shannon commented, matching her tone to his.

"Maybe with a little practice we could get our act together and take it on the road. We could bill ourselves as Gallagher and McCrae."

"What's wrong with McCrae and Gallagher?" she demanded with mock resentment.

"I'm older than you, so I'm entitled to top billing," he replied, as if that settled the matter.

The lightly teasing banter set the mood for the rest of the ride home, and by the time the pickup truck pulled into her parents' driveway, Shannon was feeling more relaxed. She had to admit the evening hadn't turned out too badly after all. At least she and Clint had gotten back on reasonably friendly footing.

Although she protested that it wasn't necessary, Clint insisted on accompanying her to the door. "My mother taught me to always see a lady safely home," he said gallantly, slipping a hand under her arm to guide her through the darkness.

As they walked across the lawn Shannon couldn't help noticing the way the moonlight cast silvery shadows on the grass, and how each star stood out in the velvet-black sky. *A night for romance.* The thought popped into her mind, unbidden. She pushed it away, but not before she felt a little pang of regret that such a lovely evening was going to waste.

When they reached the door she turned to face Clint, intending to say a quick, casual good night, and to thank him for providing transportation to and from the dinner. Her words died on her lips, though, and she caught her breath sharply as something in his expression sent a tingling weakness through her.

Several charged heartbeats of time thudded between them as their gazes clung together. She knew she ought to do something, say something, to break the spell, but she was powerless to move or speak.

She didn't resist when Clint drew her to him with a gentle strength. She went into his embrace with a feeling of inevitability. This was where she was meant to be, where she'd always belonged.

Seemingly of their own volition, her arms went around him and her fingers toyed with the thick hair at the nape of his neck. Instinctively, she pressed closer to him, her body molding itself to his lean contours. She felt a shudder course through him, as he whispered her name in a voice husky with emotion. Then, with a groan, he lowered his head so his lips could claim hers.

Although she'd fantasized many times about being kissed by Clint, the reality was infinitely sweeter than her wildest imaginings. All at once her whole world had tilted on its axis, as her emotions careened and whirled. . . .

Clint released her, almost reluctantly, and took a step or two backward so he could look down at her. She stood still, hardly daring to breathe, as his dark eyes delved deeply into hers. For the next few moments her world diminished, until nothing existed but the two of them. . . .

She was jerked sharply back to reality as the door behind her flew open.

"Thought I heard Clint's truck drive up," her father said. "Phone call for you, Shannon. It's that guy in Seattle—the one who sent flowers."

At John's words, there was a sudden, barely perceptible change in Clint's manner. She could almost feel the coldness emanating from him.

"I—I'll be right in." Shannon was thankful for the darkness that hid her flaming cheeks and trembling emotions.

"I won't keep you, if it's long distance." Clint's voice sounded tightly controlled. Shannon opened her mouth to tell him it didn't matter, but before she could utter a word he'd turned his attention to her father. "I hear Bess was ready to foal. How's she doing?"

"Great!" John replied. "She had a fine little filly about half an hour ago. Spittin' image of her ma. Come have a look."

Disheartened tears blurred Shannon's eyes as she watched Clint accompany her father out to the barn.

How could he have let that happen? Clint pounded a doubled-up fist against the steering wheel in frustration as he drove home. He'd been trying so hard to ignore the attraction he was feeling for Shannon. But she'd looked so lovely there in the moonlight, so—so kissable.

He supposed he should be relieved that that phone call had come at just the right moment to remind him she was no longer of his world. She was a city girl now, who would never be satisfied settling down on a Montana cattle ranch, and he'd do well to keep that in mind.

Chapter Seven

She was walking past the supermarket when she heard, "Look, Daddy, there's Shannon!" She glanced up to see Clint and Bethany in the parking lot next to the store. Clint was transferring several bags of groceries from a shopping cart to the back of his pickup truck.

Ignoring her father's, "Bethany, wait—" the little girl ran to Shannon and threw her arms around her with enthusiastic abandon. "I'm so glad to see you!"

"Well, I'm glad to see you too," Shannon replied, returning the embrace.

"Daddy and I are going to the Dairy Hut for ice-cream cones before we go home. We always do that after we go grocery shopping. Why don't you come with us?"

Shannon looked over Bethany's head, to meet Clint's eyes. It was obvious, from his expression, that he didn't share his daughter's enthusiasm about having her join them at the ice cream parlor. And recalling how their outing Saturday night had ended—with Clint getting all distant and remote after finding out she had a phone call from Paul—Shannon wasn't exactly thrilled with the idea of spending time in his company either. He'd certainly made it clear that kissing her had been nothing but an impulsive, unpremeditated act, one that he immediately regretted.

"I, ah, don't think—"

"Oh, *please?* We really want you to come along. Don't we, Daddy?" Bethany twisted around to look up at Clint for confirmation.

"I'm sure Shannon has other things to do," he said as he loaded the last of the groceries and closed the tailgate of the truck. A bag boy passing by wheeled the cart away.

"*Do* you?" Bethany asked, turning back to Shannon.

Shannon was about to reply that she did have other matters to attend to, but at the little girl's pleading look the polite evasion died on her lips. "No, I-I'm not really all *that* busy."

"Good. Then you can come with us," Bethany said, as if that settled the matter. Slipping one hand into Shannon's and the other into her father's, she started across the parking lot, the two grown-ups in tow. Shannon had no choice but to go along.

The ice cream parlor, next to the supermarket, was cool and quiet. "I'm having chocolate," Bethany said as they approached the counter to place their orders. "Daddy always has vanilla, but I think plain old vanilla is boring to the max, don't you?"

A little smile played around Shannon's lips. "Definitely," she replied, stealing a quick glance at Clint. "To the max."

When the teenaged counter girl handed over their cones Shannon dug her wallet out of her purse. Even though it was just an ice-cream cone, she didn't want

Clint to feel obligated to treat her just because her
company had been more or less forced on him. Clint
had the tab paid while she was still fumbling for the
right change, though. When she started to protest she
was silenced by his stony look.

"Let's sit over here," Bethany said, indicating a
table at the front of the establishment, next to the big
plate-glass window. Shannon would have preferred to
not sit where they would be so conspicuous to everyone passing by. By now it was probably all over town
that she and Clint had gone to the Ranchers' Association dinner together, and she didn't want to add fuel
to the flame. She couldn't think of any reason for
choosing another table, though.

Once they were seated Bethany said, with the
aplomb of a high-society hostess, "There now, isn't
this nice?"

Shannon managed a smile, and said, "Yes, it's very
nice," while Clint muttered something unintelligible.

Talk would have ground to a halt if it hadn't been
for the little girl, who chattered unself-consciously
about her best friend Melissa, the drill team, school.
Shannon tried to keep up her end of the conversation,
but whenever a remark was addressed directly to Clint,
he replied in clipped monosyllables.

What's eating him? Shannon wondered. Saturday
night she'd thought he was softening toward her just
a little, until a tender moment between them had been
interrupted by that phone call from Paul. What would
have happened if her father hadn't opened the door
when he did . . . ?

"And Melissa and I are going to—"

She realized Bethany had broken off in the middle

of what she was saying, and was looking at something out the window. Shannon let her own glance follow Bethany's, to see what that had claimed the child's attention.

Three boys, about Bethany's age, were coming up the street. As they approached the ice cream parlor one of the boys glanced through the window. When he spotted Bethany he crossed his eyes and stuck his tongue out. Bethany retaliated by making a face back at him.

Clint raised his eyebrows. "What was that all about?"

"That was Troy Adams. He sits next to me in school."

"Do you always greet classmates that way?"

"He's mean. He's always teasing me and pulling my hair. And sometimes he takes my pencils and other stuff and hides them." Letting her shoulders droop, she gave a sigh that would have been worthy of the heroine in an old-time melodrama.

Clint's features twisted into a concerned frown. "Picks on you, does he? We'll see about that."

Uh-oh, Shannon thought. She had a brief vision of him storming into his daughter's classroom to demand that something be done about this situation, and she knew such a course of action would do more harm than good. Besides, she had a feeling Bethany wasn't quite as annoyed by the boy's attentions as she pretended to be.

She turned to Bethany. "He probably just does that to get you to notice him. When a boy teases you that means he likes you, you know."

Bethany's eyes widened as she digested this information. "Really?"

Shannon nodded. "At least that's the way it was when I was your age."

Bethany leaned across the table. "I think he's kind of cute," she whispered to Shannon.

Shannon glanced out the window at the boy's retreating back. "He *is* cute," she agreed.

"How can I get him to stop teasing me?"

"The main thing is don't ever, under any circumstances, let him know it bothers you. And you might—" She broke off to nod a greeting to two older women walking past. One of them had done a sort of comic double take when she'd spotted Shannon sitting with Clint and Bethany, and then had excitedly nudged her companion in the ribs with her elbow. Shannon felt as if they were on display as the two women glanced in at them, smiling delightedly.

"You might try being extra nice to him," she continued when the two ladies had gone on. "That'll really throw him off guard. He won't know what you're up to. He'll think you're cooking up something to get even with him."

Bethany giggled. "That'll serve him right."

Shannon laughed too, but when she stole a glance at Clint she saw that he hadn't cracked a smile. Obviously, he didn't like her giving advice about boys to his daughter. He probably thought she was putting ideas into Bethany's head. Darn it, though, she didn't have a mother and there were times when a little girl needed someone to talk things over with. She couldn't imagine the good-hearted but staid Thelma Kruger having this conversation with her young charge. Still, she decided it was time to switch to another topic.

"I heard you went on a major clothes-shopping spree a while back." That seemed safe enough. All little girls loved new clothes.

"Did I ever!" Bethany confirmed, rolling her eyes. "I got a whole bunch of new stuff because Thelma said I'm growing like a weed. There was this pink T-shirt with merry-go-round horses on it that Thelma didn't think I should have because it wasn't 'practical'" —she made a little face to demonstrate her feelings about practicality—"but I really, really wanted it, so she finally gave in. It's *sooo* pretty. And I got some new sweaters, and a pair of boots . . ."

As Bethany described the new additions to her wardrobe, Shannon couldn't help admiring the delicate features, the animated sparkle in the dark eyes. Her heart contracted at the thought that if Clint hadn't married someone else, their child might look like this. She realized she was becoming awfully fond of Bethany— and not just because she was Clint's daughter. She was a sweet, lovable little girl, and Shannon knew she would miss her a lot when she returned to Seattle.

Finishing his ice cream, Clint got to his feet. "I hate to break this up but if we don't get home and get those groceries put away, everything's going to spoil."

"I need to get going, too," Shannon said, standing up. "I have some errands to take care of."

Bethany popped the last of her ice-cream cone into her mouth and turned to Shannon. "I'm going to try what you said—being extra nice to Troy. Can I call you and let you know how it works out?"

"Of course. But you don't have to wait for a reason,

you know. You can call me any time you just want to talk.'' She turned to Clint with a brief, ''Thanks for the ice cream.'' She could almost feel his scowl as she hurried out of the ice cream parlor.

Shannon shook her head in dismay as she watched the riders go through their paces. It was hard to believe this was the same team that, less than two weeks ago, had taken first place in the drill competition in Fremont. Today they looked like a bunch of beginners who had never been on horseback before.

She had to admit she was as much to blame as anyone for the way the practice session was going. She was distracted and out of sorts, and was probably communicating her own feelings to the team.

She was aware, of course, that the reason for her mood was slouched on a seat up in the bleachers just behind her, watching the proceedings. For a while after the drill competition Clint had stopped attending the practice sessions, apparently satisfied that Shannon had things well in hand. But now he was back, looking more disapproving than before. She tried to ignore him, with little success. She could feel his gaze boring into her.

''Listen up, everybody,'' she called out. ''I want you to go over that last maneuver again. And try not to lose your rhythm when you come out of the Texas Star and start into the Figure Eight.''

She watched critically as they guided their horses through the steps, trying their best to follow her instructions. Something still wasn't right. Their timing was way off, their movements jerky and uncoordinated. She waved her arm, signaling them to stop.

"Let's begin again, and see if it goes a little better," she said, without much conviction.

After several false starts, the team finally got through a shaky version of the maneuver. Shannon resisted the urge to glance over her shoulder to see if Clint was watching.

What in the world was he doing here? Clint asked himself. He'd used the excuse that he had to bring Bethany's horse home in the trailer—but that was no reason to stay for the entire session. He could just as easily have dropped her and the horse off and then come back when practice was over. Deep down, he knew he was here because this was where Shannon was—even though every vestige of common sense he had left was telling him that after the disastrous end to Saturday evening's outing, the smartest thing he could do would be to stay as far away from her as possible.

For that one evening he'd allowed himself to be lulled into forgetting that she was only here temporarily, that soon she'd be going back to Seattle. *And to the other guy,* a little voice inside him added.

So why *was* he here, behaving like a lovesick high school kid? He was as bad as that Troy kid in Bethany's class. He could only surmise that a previously latent streak of masochism had suddenly surfaced, making him want to twist the knife in the wound. *". . . Like a moth to a flame . . ."* The phrase from an old country-western song ran through his head.

He'd honestly *tried* to put her out of his mind, but distracting memories had kept popping into his consciousness at odd moments. He'd be clearing a water hole or repairing an irrigation pipe, and the next thing he knew he'd be picturing how she'd looked in that clingy blue dress. And even if he could erase the image from his thoughts, his body reacted with a treacherous longing he was powerless to resist. Against his will, he kept recalling the way she'd felt in his arms, the taste of her lips, warm and soft, under his . . .

He muttered an oath. He had to stop this. She wasn't for him, and the sooner he got that through his head the better off he'd be.

After several more unsuccessful run-throughs, Shannon was ready to concede that, considering the current mood that hung over the arena, continuing the practice session was an exercise in futility. "I think maybe we're all trying too hard," she called out. "Why don't we give it up for today? Practice as usual Thursday evening."

There was a chorus of assents as the riders fell out of formation. Apparently everyone else was as relieved as she was to have the embarrassing session over with.

Clint felt a stab of guilt when he saw that practice was breaking up early. He had to admit it was just barely possible that it was his fault. Things might have gone along more smoothly if he'd stayed away.

As he left the arena he spotted Bethany and two of her teammates gathered around her horse, Sandy. Bethany had the animal's foot raised and was examining his hoof.

"Let's get Sandy loaded up so we can get going," he called to her.

"Daddy, I think he has a rock caught in his hoof," she said, releasing the foot and leading the little bay horse over to him. "Would you take a look at it?"

He watched the horse's gait with a practiced eye. "Looks all right to me."

"*No,* Daddy, I think he's in pain."

Already ashamed of his earlier behavior, Clint was anxious to get away before he did anything else stupid. "I'll take care of it when we get home," he said.

"But it hurts him *now.*" Her large, expressive eyes seemed on the verge of filling with tears.

"Oh, all right," he said, relenting. "Why don't you run over to the tack shed and get me a hoof pick."

"I looked in there a little while ago—when I first noticed he was limping—and I couldn't find one."

Clint tried unsuccessfully to stifle an impatient sigh. "I guess I'll have to find it for you." He headed for the structure behind the arena, muttering, "It was probably right under your nose."

As the riders left the ring Shannon stayed behind, jotting down notes about the changes she'd made. She didn't want to go outside until she was sure Clint was gone. She didn't feel up to another encounter with him. She glanced up from her clipboard as Cody came back into the arena.

"Shannon, what about that martingale?" he asked.

"Martingale?" she echoed vaguely, still concentrating on her notes.

"You know. You said why didn't I try using one during practice, to keep Pete from tossing his head back."

"Oh." She forced her attention back to the present. "There's one in the tack shed. You can go and get it."

"I saw it out there, but it's on a nail way up high. I can't reach it."

"I'll get if for you," she said, putting her clipboard aside. As she headed for the back exit to the arena, she reflected that hunting up the piece of equipment for Cody would keep her out of Clint's way until he left.

But when she entered the small building she found Clint rummaging through the items on the shelf and mumbling to himself, "There are usually at least half a dozen hoof picks lying around. Where did they all go . . ." He glanced around to see who had come in, and frowned when he saw that it was Shannon.

Her first impulse was to back out of the shed, but she told herself not to be ridiculous. She had as much right as Clint to be here. She'd just get what she came for and be on her way. She edged past him, scanning the various items hanging on nails on the wall, as she searched for the strip of leather with metal rings on one end.

Her forehead furrowed in concentration, she hardly noticed the muffled sound outside the shed. She whirled around, her expression puzzled, as the door to the shed swung shut with a soft little *click*.

Chapter Eight

The shaft of sunlight coming in the doorway was blotted out, throwing the interior of the small building into semidarkness.

Shannon's first thought was a vague feeling of surprise. She hadn't noticed that it was especially windy today—at least, not windy enough to blow the door shut.

Automatically, Clint turned from rummaging through the items on the shelf and reached over to open it. "Seems to be stuck," he muttered, pushing against it with his shoulder. It refused to budge.

"Here, let me see if I can do it," Shannon said.

Clint resisted the urge to ask what made her think she could get the door open if he couldn't. He'd already caused enough trouble for one day. He moved aside to allow her to try.

She rattled the knob several times with no results. "Hey, is anybody out there?" she called out.

When there was no reply, Clint stepped back up to the door and banged on it, shouting, "Bethany! Somebody! We're locked in!"

The only answer was complete silence.

The single window in the shed faced the opposite

direction from the arena, looking out on an empty field, so it was impossible to see if anyone was around. But all the team members couldn't have gone, Shannon reasoned. Bethany wouldn't leave without Clint, and Cody would be waiting for her to return with the martingale. And many of the kids often hung around after drill practice to do some practicing on their own. But the arena was far enough away from the tack shed that she knew she could shout herself hoarse and not be heard. It could be quite a while before anyone even missed them and thought to come looking for them.

All at once, as Shannon became uneasily aware of what a small space they were confined in, for no telling how long, something close to panic shot through her. She didn't relish being shut in here with someone so moody and unpredictable she never knew where she stood with him from one moment to the next.

Saturday night, for instance; at first he'd seemed uncomfortable and ill at ease. She'd supposed it was because he'd resented having her thrust at him that way. Later on, though, when he'd pulled her close and kissed her, he'd been a completely different person. At the time, she hadn't stopped to analyze what was happening between them—whether he was actually beginning to feel something for her, or was just under the influence of the moonlight and the soft spring evening. She'd simply savored the sheer joy of being in his arms. . . .

Clint apparently grasped their predicament at the same time as Shannon, judging by the sudden expression of dismay that came over his features. He didn't appear to be any happier about the two of them being trapped together in a six-by-eight-foot shed than she was. He paced a few steps, which was as far as his long strides would take him in the small area, then took off his hat and ran a hand through his hair in an impatient gesture. The thought crossed Shannon's mind that this was like being shut in with a large, very nervous, wild beast.

Replacing his hat and thrusting his hands into his pockets, Clint turned to stare at the small, high window. What was on his mind? Shannon wondered. His large frame would never fit through there . . .

"If you think I'm going to climb through that little-bitty opening, you can forget it," she said firmly, as she sensed what he was thinking. Even being trapped in here was preferable to the indignity of allowing Clint to boost her up to the window, and then knowing he was watching her as she wiggled out.

"Couldn't you kick the door open, or—or something?"

He shook his head. "That only works on television."

She shot him a chilly look, as if to say this was all his fault, if he wouldn't even *try*. "Well, then, I guess we'll just have to wait until someone misses us." She hoped to convey, by her offhand tone, that although she found the idea less than appealing, she was prepared to tough it out if he was.

Clint jammed his hands further into his pockets and rested his tall frame against the wall. Sighing deeply, Shannon shrugged and folded her arms, in a gesture intended to indicate her complete indifference to his presence. Neither of them said a word, as the seconds lengthened into minutes. The only sounds were birds singing somewhere off in the distance, and the buzzing of a bee just outside the door. How long were they going to have to stand around like this, pretending to ignore each other? Shannon wondered.

Her glance darted about the room, at the wall, the shelf, the window, anywhere to avoid meeting Clint's eyes . . .

She spotted the martingale she had come into the shed to get. The leather contraption was hanging on a nail up toward the ceiling, far out of her reach. If she could just find something to stand on . . .

She noticed a small wooden stepladder, about two feet high, tucked away in the corner under the shelf. It didn't look too sturdy, she thought as she pulled it out, but it would have to do.

Clint's brows drew together in a frown as he recognized her intentions. ''What do you need up there?'' he asked, straightening. ''I'll get it for you.''

''That's quite all right,'' she murmured. ''I can do it myself.'' She realized she sounded childish and petty—it would have been a simple matter to just tell him she wanted the martingale, and let him get it. He'd barely even have to stretch. But after the way he'd been acting, she had no intention of asking him for help.

''Hey, be careful!'' he said with alarm, noticing how the ladder wobbled when she climbed up onto the narrow top step and reached upward. He put a hand on her arm to steady her, but she brushed it away with an impatient gesture. The quick, jerky motion was all that was needed to start the ladder teetering precariously. She felt it begin to topple just as her fingers closed around the martingale.

She struggled unsuccessfully to maintain her balance. Her heart slammed against her ribs when she realized she was falling and there wasn't a thing she could do about it. An involuntary cry escaped her as she braced herself for the impact.

All at once a strong, protective arm came around her waist, steadying her, and she felt herself being lowered to her feet while the ladder tumbled harmlessly in the other direction.

After the surge of adrenaline that had rushed through her veins, her legs felt weak and rubbery, as if they might not support her. She gave in to the urge to rest in that comforting embrace as she drew in several deep, calming breaths. She'd pull away in a few seconds, she told herself. As soon as she stopped shaking . . .

Clint had reacted instinctively when he'd seen Shannon start to fall. There hadn't been time to think things over. He'd simply put an arm around her waist and lifted her from the ladder. Once he set her down it seemed natural to continue to hold her for a few moments—just to give her time to pull herself together.

He was unprepared, though, for the sudden rush of emotions that surged through him when she leaned against him in that trusting way. With what vestige of rational thought still remained, he knew he should release her now that she was out of danger.

But he couldn't seem to make his limbs obey his will. Hardly aware of what he was doing, he flattened both hands against Shannon's back and gently pulled her even closer. She came to him willingly, with a soft little sigh that went straight to his heart.

A warning signal went off in the back of his mind,

reminding him that this could only lead to trouble. He managed to ignore it, though, as his emotions over-ruled his common sense. All at once there was no world beyond the boundaries of the small shed and the warm, desirable woman in his arms. Time stood still as he continued to hold her, feeling her heart beating against his chest, synchronizing with his own. He savored the way her slender curves fit into his embrace as if she belonged there, the way the top of her head came to just under his chin, the slight, sweet scent that clung to her hair . . .

It must be getting stuffy in here, he thought—he seemed to be having trouble breathing. Swallowing to ease the dryness in his throat, he put a callused finger under Shannon's chin and tilted it up so he could look deep into her eyes. What he saw there mirrored his own emotions.

One hand slid up to the nape of her neck, where he threaded his fingers through her silky hair. Then his mouth met hers, and a feeling of inevitability took possession of him.

Had she been able to think clearly, Shannon might have been shocked at the eagerness of her response, but her senses were in such a whirl that she was aware only of an intoxicating warmth that spread through her entire being. For what could have been a second—or an eternity—time lost all meaning.

When they finally drew apart Clint dragged a ragged breath into his lungs. "Shannon . . ." he rasped. But then his words died away, as if he were in a state of bewilderment over what had just happened.

That was just as well, Shannon thought, as she willed her racing pulse to settle down. With her emotions still swimming, she wasn't ready to talk about what was happening between them. Right now she had all she could do to regain her equilibrium and cling to the ever-shifting edge of a world that had suddenly slipped off its axis. Her mouth still tingled from his kiss, and her skin, even under the material of her shirt, burned where he'd touched her. She needed time to pull herself together.

Besides, she was afraid to discuss the matter of *Where do we go from here?* If Clint had merely reacted to a sudden physical attraction, the result of their being unexpectedly thrown together—well, she'd have to deal with that later, but not now. Not while she was still enveloped in this soft glow, while this melting sweetness still permeated every fiber of her being.

Clint started to reach out to her but caught himself in mid-gesture and let his hands drop to his sides, as if he didn't trust himself to touch her again. He took a few steps backwards.

Shannon found herself suddenly shy in his presence, unable to think of a thing to say. After what had just taken place, they couldn't just stand there discussing such mundane matters as the weather or the price of yearling calves. Would she ever be able to behave normally around him again?

"It-it's awfully warm in here," she said as the silence between them stretched out. She fanned herself with her hand.

"Ah . . . warm. Yes. It's very warm."

That pretty well exhausted that conversational topic, Shannon thought. *Now what?* She glanced up at Clint through lowered lashes, trying to gauge his feelings. Was he sorry about what had happened?

He shifted from one foot to the other, uncertainly. Then, with an air of having come to a decision, he pulled her back into his arms. She went willingly, with no hesitancy, as if that was exactly where she wanted to be.

This time there was none of the urgency that had marked their previous embrace. His mouth took possession of hers slowly, gently, in a kiss of such incredible sweetness that her insides seemed to be melting. He pulled away long enough to draw in a deep breath, then began teasing her lips in a way that sent delicious little tremors through her.

Shannon was sure she could have stayed in Clint's arms forever, his mouth caressing hers. All too soon, though, they heard the sound of approaching hoof-beats. "Daddy, are you in there?" Bethany's voice came through the thin walls of the building. "What's taking you so long?"

Clint brushed his lips across Shannon's one last time before calling out, "We're locked in." Slowly, reluctantly, he released her. "We can't get the door open."

There was a muffled conversation outside the shed, as if a hurried consultation was being held, and a few seconds later they could hear the doorknob being rattled. Then the late-afternoon sunlight slanted in as the door swung open to reveal Bethany and several other team members peering in at them curiously.

"I don't know why you couldn't get it open," Bethany said, while Shannon and Clint blinked in the sudden brightness. "It opened just fine for me."

Clint shot a speculative glance at his daughter, but her expression was as guileless as a baby's. He started to say something, then shook his head, apparently thinking better of it.

"That door has always been tricky," one of the other riders offered helpfully. "Sometimes it locks by itself when it's slammed, and you can only get it open from the outside."

"But we didn't slam it," Shannon said. "It just swung shut."

"Must have been the wind," someone else put in.

Shannon was about to point out that it didn't seem that windy today, when Clint asked, "Couldn't you hear us calling?"

The rescuers exchanged glances, then Bethany spoke up. "We were all over on the other side of the arena. We didn't hear a thing."

"Well, let's get out of here before we get locked in again," Clint said. Stepping aside, he held out one hand in a gesture that indicated he was waiting for Shannon to go before him.

As she exited the shed, she remembered that she still had the martingale in her hand. "Oh, this is for you, Cody," she said, holding the strip of leather out to him.

"Daddy, did you get the hoof pick?" Bethany asked.

"I couldn't find one," Clint replied in a preoccupied tone. "They all seem to have disappeared."

"That's okay. Sandy's foot is all right now. I guess the rock must have worked its way out."

When Clint didn't reply, Shannon glanced behind her to see what he found so absorbing. He was examining the doorknob, twisting it in both directions experimentally. "Funny how it locked by itself," he muttered under his breath.

The riders exchanged glances, and Bethany reddened slightly.

"No harm done," Clint said with an offhanded shrug. As they walked away from the shed he put a hand on Shannon's shoulder and leaned down to whisper in her ear. "I think we've been set up."

"Set up!" she echoed. "But what—"

"Shh." He nodded toward the riders ahead of them. All at once everything started to fall into place—the trumped-up excuses for sending both of them to the shed, the "defective" lock. Shannon was almost embarrassed at how easily she'd fallen for their tricks. She wouldn't be surprised to discover the little scamps had even hidden all the hoof picks just to keep Clint in the shed long enough for her to get there.

She supposed she ought to give them a stern talking-to. They should be made to understand that they couldn't go around manipulating people that way. She couldn't find it in her heart to be angry with them, though. Not when the memory of those kisses she and Clint had shared was enough to start her senses skidding erratically.

Chapter Nine

The gathered skirt of Shannon's white peasant-style dress whirled around her slim legs as she came down the stairs and pirouetted gracefully.

Maureen nodded her approval. "You look absolutely lovely, dear."

"It's easy to see who'll be the prettiest young woman at this shindig," John said.

"It's just barely possible you might be a bit prejudiced," Shannon replied with a smile. "You two look pretty good yourselves, you know." Her mother's delicate coloring was heightened by the soft pink of her crinkled cotton dress, and her dad was trim and handsome in his western shirt and dress-up jeans. Even the cast that replaced one shiny, ornate boot, rather than detracting from his appearance, gave him a somewhat rakish air.

"And that necklace you're wearing is perfect with your dress," Maureen said. She leaned toward Shannon to take a closer look at the dainty silver pendant, set with a turquoise stone. "I don't remember seeing it before. Where did you get it?"

Shannon toyed with the delicate chain around her neck. "I-I've had it for a long time," she replied evasively.

John wrinkled his brow in concentration as he surveyed his daughter's outfit. "Didn't you have a dress like that when you were a teenager? You know I don't pay much attention to feminine doodads, but I seem to remember you in something white, that came down off your shoulders, just like what you're wearing now. I think it was at your sixteenth birthday party."

Coloring slightly, Shannon lowered her eyes. Thoughts of that long-ago event brought conflicting emotions. The reason this dress had caught her attention was because it *was* similar to the one she'd worn that evening ten years ago, the one she'd chosen especially to open Clint's eyes to the fact that she was no longer a child.

When she'd spotted the garment last week in the window of a shop called The Western Lady, on a side street in Liberty, she'd gazed at it longingly. It would be perfect to wear to the Murdochs' anniversary party. But then she shook her head and continued on her way, as she reminded herself she wouldn't have much opportunity to wear it after the party, especially once she returned to Seattle.

Later on, as she and Maureen were discussing the upcoming event, she'd asked casually, "By the way, who's coming to this party?"

"Oh, the usual crowd," Maureen had replied. "All the close neighbors."

Shannon understood that in this land of vast stretches of emptiness, "close neighbors" was a relative term, and was usually meant to include everyone within at least a twenty- or thirty-mile radius.

"Viv Murdoch even mentioned that Clint might be there," Maureen went on. "She called him personally to invite him. She couldn't pin him down to a definite answer, but he did at least promise to think about it. You know, we're always trying to get him to get out and circulate, but he keeps to himself so much these days.''

The next time Shannon was in town she couldn't resist walking past The Western Lady—just to see if the dress was still in the window. Surely it would have been sold by now, she told herself.

But there it was, beckoning to her. It wouldn't hurt to just go in and take a closer look, she thought. It probably wasn't even her size, and that would settle the matter once and for all.

''My, aren't you the lucky one,'' the clerk said as Shannon emerged from the fitting room a short time later. ''That dress fits you so well it could have been made for you. It was a specialty item,'' she explained. ''We just got the one in.''

Shannon twisted and turned in front of the three-way mirror, examining her reflection from all angles. The dress did fit perfectly. And, without undue conceit, she had to admit it looked darned good on her. The creamy white fabric set off her tan to perfection, and the wide silver belt, which reflected the touches of silver around the off-the-shoulder neckline, emphasized her slender waist.

''I'll take it,'' she heard herself saying.

Now why did I do that? she wondered as she left the shop carrying her purchase. What was she trying to do by buying a dress so much like that one she'd had when she was sixteen—turn back the clock?

Even if Clint did show up at the Murdochs' party, and even that was uncertain—he'd merely said he'd think about it—nothing would really have changed. Did she honestly believe that after one look at her he was going to realize what he'd given up ten years ago, and suddenly declare his undying love? *Get real, girl,* she told herself. That sort of thing only happened in the romantic old movies that turned up on late-night television.

So just what *did* she hope to accomplish?

Driving home, she had to admit she wasn't really sure. Maybe she simply wanted to erase the memory of that long-ago evening, when she'd poured her heart out to Clint and he'd taken her girlish hopes and dreams and quietly ripped them to shreds.

Oh, he'd been as gentle as he could have been under the circumstances. She was certain that to this day he had no inkling of what his words had done to her. Still, she hadn't known it was possible to hurt so badly. Even after ten years, just the thought of her humiliation and disappointment was enough to bring on a sharp stab of pain, like an old wound that still ached on rainy days.

Was she wrong to want to replace that memory with another, pleasanter one, a memory that wouldn't cause that deep, wrenching hurt?

At least Clint had finally acknowledged that she was a grown woman, and not just the kid next door. That much was clear from the way he'd kissed her when they'd gotten trapped together in the tack shed. She'd run into him in town a few days after that episode, and she'd detected a certain glint in his eyes that told her he was genuinely pleased to see her.

"I was just on my way over to Edna Mae's," he'd said, casually linking his arm through hers. "How

about coming along with me?'' She couldn't have refused even if she'd wanted to—not with his touch
causing those odd little flutters in the pit of her
stomach.

Over pie and coffee at Edna Mae's diner, they'd
talked of inconsequential matters, but beneath the light
conversation had been the underlying awareness of
that sudden, overwhelming electricity that had sprung
up between them. It was as if neither of them knew
quite how to handle this new development.

Clint was attracted to her, that at least was obvious—but was a physical attraction enough to break
through the wall he had built up around himself?

If he did come to the Murdochs' party, at least they
could share a dance or two together, a little mild flirt-
ing, maybe even a good-night kiss. But would that be
enough for her? Would it see her through the lonely
times after she returned to Seattle, when she longed
for him so badly it was almost a physical ache?

It would have to be, she told herself. In time she
might even be able to put him out of her mind, fall in
love with someone else, and lead a more or less normal life.

Fat chance, something inside her scoffed.

John's voice broke into Shannon's thoughts. ''If
you two are ready, may I have the honor of escorting
my two favorite ladies to the party?'' With a courtly
little bow, he held out one arm to Maureen and another
to Shannon.

Shannon and her parents were greeted by the
mouth-watering aromas of roasting meat and barbecue
sauce as soon as they arrived at the Murdoch ranch.

The Murdochs liked to do things on a lavish scale, and the side of beef that was to be the main course for the sumptuous buffet had been sizzling over the coals for hours.

A festive air hung over the Murdochs' spacious backyard. Soft music floated across the patio and colored lanterns reflected their soft, shimmery light in the swimming pool.

Shannon felt a sense of pleasant anticipation. In a setting like this, anything could happen. It was the same feeling she used to have when she was a child and awoke on Christmas morning, wondering what delights the day held . . .

The same feeling she'd had on her sixteenth birthday, as she'd looked forward to her party that evening. It was to be an outdoor barbecue, much like the Murdochs' anniversary party, but on a smaller scale. Although most of the guests would be Shannon's teenage friends, she'd extracted a promise from Clint that he'd at least stop by for a ''birthday dance'' with her.

She'd spent the first half of the evening watching for him, in an agony of anticipation. When she had just about given up, there he was. She'd spotted him across the patio, making his way toward her. He *had* come!

There was no denying, from the expression of admiration in his eyes, that he was at last beginning to see her as a woman, not just as the little neighbor girl. Her heart had leapt into her throat as she'd watched him draw nearer. All at once everything around her faded away—the other guests, the murmur of conversation, the music.

Then he was standing in front of her. ''I've come

for that dance you promised me.'' Even now she could recall how the rich timbre of his voice had been like gentle fingers massaging her spine.

''Let's go someplace where we can be by ourselves for a little while,'' she said. Taking his hand, she'd pulled him around to the side of the house, where a grove of trees offered them some privacy. He went along without protest, smiling indulgently, as if wondering what kind of deviltry she was cooking up now.

''Now then,'' she said when they were alone, ''I'm ready for our dance.''

''First let me give you your present.'' He took a small box from his pocket and held it out to her.

Her fingers trembled with excitement as she undid the wrappings. ''Ohhh.'' She gave a soft little exclamation when she saw the exquisite turquoise pendant nestled in a bed of white tissue paper. She held it up by its delicate chain, turning it this way and that, admiring the way the silver border twinkled when the moonlight caught it.

''Oh, Clint, it's beautiful!'' She looked up at him, her eyes shining. ''Put it on me, please.'' She handed the piece of jewelry back to him and whirled around, holding her long thick hair up out of the way with one hand.

Her skin tingled where his fingers brushed the back of her neck as he fumbled with the pendant's clasp. Once he had it fastened she released her hair to let it fall in an auburn cloud around her bare shoulders. Her heart pounding, she turned to face him. This would be the perfect time to tell him what was in her heart. Surely he must be feeling what she felt . . .

Shannon's reminiscence was interrupted as Viv and

Brady Murdoch swept down on her and her parents to greet them enthusiastically. ''My, it's nice to see you again, Shannon,'' Viv said. ''You really ought to move back here. Seattle is so far away. I can't imagine why you'd prefer Washington to Montana.''

Shannon was spared the necessity of coming up with an appropriate reply when several of her friends spotted her. In no time she was drawn into the group and whisked off to where the younger guests were congregating.

Chapter Ten

Clint could hear music and laughter as he got out of the pickup truck and walked around to the Murdochs' backyard. He'd been fighting a battle with himself ever since Viv had called to let him know how disappointed she and Brady would be if he didn't come to their party. The habit of keeping to himself had become so deeply ingrained that he almost turned down the invitation automatically, but then he'd caught himself. It would probably do him good to get out among people again. It had been six years since his marriage broke up. He couldn't stay a hermit the rest of his life.

He tried to tell himself that the fact that Shannon would be at the party had nothing to do with his decision to go. Deep inside, though, he knew it had everything to do with it. She'd been on his mind constantly, ever since that day he'd run into her at the hardware store. Wasn't it time he stopped fighting what was in his heart? Just because his marriage had turned out so badly, that was no reason to mistrust all women. Maybe he was being given a second chance— a chance to exorcise the ghosts of the past and start over.

"Clint, glad to see you made it." Brady Murdoch stepped up and welcomed him with a hearty hand-shake and a slap on the back. "Make yourself at home. Food is over that way." He gestured in the direction of the buffet. "Just help yourself."

They made small talk until Brady's attention was claimed by another guest. "I'll just wander around and see who's here," Clint said, although, of course, there was only one person he was really interested in seeing.

He headed in the direction his host indicated, edging his way around the couples dancing on the patio. To all appearances, he was merely strolling along casu-ally, not looking for anyone in particular. He had his hands in his pockets, and he nodded to several people who called out greetings to him.

He was halfway across the patio when he spotted her. He halted in his progress and stood transfixed, something stirring deep inside him. Without warning the memories of that other party, ten years ago, came flooding back. She'd been dressed much the same way that night, in a white dress that came down off her shoulders, revealing an expanse of smooth, tanned skin. Even the pendant that hung from a silver chain around her neck looked very similar to the one he'd given her, but he was too far away to be sure. He squinted, trying to make it out.

Even from this distance he could see the animated sparkle in her eyes, as if she were expecting something wonderful to happen. She'd had that same sparkle the night of her birthday party. He recalled her air of sup-pressed excitement as she'd taken his hand and led him around to that grove of trees.

He'd had no idea what she'd had in mind. Looking

back, he saw that he should have realized what was coming—she'd certainly sent out enough signals. But to his everlasting regret, he hadn't picked up on them. He'd thought she was simply indulging in her flair for the dramatic.

After he'd fastened the chain around her neck and she'd turned back to face him, he'd been taken completely by surprise when she'd twined her arms around him. Stunned, he'd twisted out of her embrace and backed away as if he'd come in contact with something hot. "Shannon, what are you doing!"

Undaunted, she had closed the space between them and put her arms around him again. "You must know by now that I love you. Oh, I know what you're going to say—that I'm too young to know my own mind. But I'm not. I've always loved you. I think it's time I brought my feelings out into the open."

With resolute firmness, he'd reached around and untwined her arms. "Don't *do* that. If anybody saw us, what would they think?"

Her smile was confident. "They'd think, *Isn't that wonderful! Clint and Shannon are in love.*"

He made another attempt to reason with her. "Shannon, listen to me—"

She silenced him with a finger to his lips. "Oh, I don't expect you to do anything about it now. I realize I still have a lot of growing up to do. I have to finish high school and go to college. But I want to make sure you know I love you, before it's too late. I don't want you finding someone else . . ."

It was too late already, but how could he tell her that? How could he tell her he'd met someone while he was away at college? Already Valerie, with her polished, big-city ways and her air of sophistication, was a fire in his blood.

Putting his hands on Shannon's shoulders so he could hold her at arm's length, he'd tried to explain to her that what she felt for him was just infatuation, that there could never be anything between them but friendship and that eventually she'd meet someone else . . .

As he'd rattled off the pat phrases, he told himself he was doing the right thing. It wouldn't be fair to give her any false encouragement. Still, he couldn't suppress the rush of guilt he felt when he saw the sparkle go out of her eyes, as if someone had turned off a light switch.

With a little choking sound, she'd twisted out of his grasp. He didn't call her back as she turned and ran from him, her quick, angry movements causing her full skirt to whirl out around her. What good would it do? There was nothing else he could say that would ease the hurt he'd caused her.

When he left the grove of trees and went back to the party Shannon was nowhere to be seen. He wondered if she was up in her room crying. He felt *something* was expected of him, but he wasn't quite sure what. It occurred to him that probably the kindest thing he could do for her right now would be to make himself scarce. He was reluctant to leave, though, until he was sure she was all right.

Eventually she'd reappeared, and before long she was the center of a group of her friends, laughing and joking with them. With her head held high, she had the air of a young princess. Except for the faint tinge of pink in her cheeks and the telltale glitter in her eyes, there was nothing to indicate that anything out of the ordinary had taken place.

He'd noticed she wasn't wearing the turquoise pendant.

Shannon's laughter, low and musical, floated across the patio, breaking into Clint's remembrances, forcing his thoughts back to the present.

As he stood watching her she turned, smiling, to respond to something one of the other guests had said to her. At the slight movement the touches of silver trim around the neckline of her dress twinkled in the moonlight. She looked so lovely that his heart twisted inside him at the thought of what he'd so casually thrown away. He wondered if it was too late to make amends.

He didn't flatter himself that she'd been pining away for him all these years—she seemed to have gotten on with her life quite well without him. Still, her response to his kisses had left no doubt that a spark of the love she'd once offered him still remained. Was there enough left of that spark that it could be rekindled into a flame?

Maybe if they had more time to find out . . . But she would be returning to Seattle in a few weeks. Could he possibly persuade her to change her mind about leaving—at least until they had time to explore their feelings more closely?

But that wasn't going to happen if he continued to stand here doing nothing, like a bump on a log. It was time for some positive action.

Having given himself this pep talk, he took a deep breath and squared his shoulders resolutely. He couldn't seem to control the churning in his stomach, though. *Just keep your cool*, he told himself. *All you have to do is walk up to her and ask her to dance.* He had a feeling she wouldn't turn him down. And once she was in his arms—well, he'd just let nature take its course, and see what developed. *Now get moving, man.*

But he'd taken only two or three steps when he slowed to a halt, frowning, as a figure detached itself from the crowd and approached Shannon from the other direction. He muttered under his breath.

The fellow leaned close to Shannon—much *too* close, Clint thought—to say something in her ear. It was obvious, from the way he glanced toward the dance floor, that he was asking her to dance. In the space of a few seconds a multitude of emotions raced through Clint's mind, from jealousy to a feeling of resignation. What had made him think he had even a ghost of a chance, with so many other guys buzzing around her like flies around honey? Thank goodness he'd come to his senses before he made a complete fool of himself.

Shannon smiled up at the eager young man, nodding her acceptance. Clint watched this pantomime with a sinking sensation. He had the feeling that many of the other guests were watching him and Shannon, and that they were the topic of much interest and speculation.

He rocked back on his heels slightly while he considered how to make his retreat without being too obvious. He hoped to give the impression, to anyone looking on, that he'd merely strolled out onto the patio to watch the couples dancing. And having done that, he was ready to move on.

Afterward, he was never quite sure just what had stopped him from turning and walking away. Maybe it was the thought of someone else putting his arms around Shannon and holding her close as they swayed in time to the soft, romantic music. Was he going to just stand around and let that happen?

With a glint of determination in his eye, he reached Shannon in a few quick strides and planted himself squarely in front of her, just as the other guy was putting his hand on her arm. She glanced up to see who was blocking her way, and her eyes widened in surprise. Clint knew this was no time for foot-dragging. If he didn't move fast he was going to make an even bigger mistake than the one he'd made ten years ago.

"I believe this is our dance." He hadn't planned on saying that. It just popped out. Without waiting for a reply, he put an arm around Shannon's waist and drew her onto the dance floor. As he took her in his arms he could hardly believe he'd actually done that. He hadn't acted so impulsively in years, although in his younger days he'd had a reputation for being rash and impetuous. It had been part of his nature to act first and worry about the consequences later, until his disastrous marriage had taught him to be cautious, to weigh each action carefully before rushing into anything.

Shannon barely had time to cast a quick, apologetic glance over her shoulder at her would-be partner before giving herself up to the sheer bliss of being held in Clint's arms. Resting her cheek against his chest, she gave a long, contented sigh. Eventually, as her pulse rate began to slow down to normal, she glanced up at him questioningly, through her eyelashes.

Clint's eyes met hers. "I'm sorry if I interrupted something, but I've been waiting ten years for this dance."

"Ten years?" Shannon echoed.

"Since the night of your sixteenth birthday. Don't you remember? You promised me a dance, but then you ran off before I had a chance to collect on that promise."

Did she *remember*! Didn't he know she had relived that evening almost every day for the last ten years? "After the way I threw myself at you, I didn't know what else to do but run away," she murmured, lowering her gaze. "It must have been terribly embarrassing for you, having this little sixteen-year-old girl flinging herself at you."

"No, actually it was very flattering. Looking back, I can see I could have handled the situation better than I did. I—I'm afraid I was caught off guard, though. I wasn't expecting anything like that."

"Surely you must have had some idea that I had a major crush on you." She made an attempt to keep her tone light. "After all, I'd been your constant shadow almost ever since I was old enough to walk. I'm sure I must have been a real pain, trailing around after you all the time."

"I can't recall that I minded all that much. It just seemed natural. We *were* close neighbors, and our folks were good friends—I guess I thought of you like a little sister. I should have realized what was happening, though."

"Don't blame yourself. I'm afraid I was incurably romantic," she said in a rueful tone.

"All the same, I wish I'd been a little more understanding. I must have sounded unbearably pompous and stuffy, with my pat little speech." He paused briefly, as if weighing his words, before going on. "If you'd been a little older, and if I hadn't been involved with Valerie . . ." He hated bringing up the subject of his former wife, but it was something that couldn't be ignored. If Valerie hadn't been in the picture he might not have been so quick to tell Shannon they could never be anything but friends. "In any event, would you accept an apology that's ten years too late?"

"Only if you'll accept *my* apology for putting you in such an embarrassing position that night."

"Deal."

Shannon let her breath out slowly, in a sigh of relief. Thank goodness they'd gotten *that* out into the open and cleared the air.

Clint glanced down as if he were studying her. Just as she was beginning to feel a little uncomfortable under his scrutiny, he commented thoughtfully, "That necklace you're wearing—it looks like the one I gave you."

"It is," she replied with a little smile.

"I'm surprised you still have it." Although his tone was casual, it was obvious he was pleased.

"It's one of my favorite pieces of jewelry." That much was true. He didn't need to know that after she'd fled to her room in tears she'd torn it from her neck, breaking the clasp, and flung it into her wastebasket. A few days later, after some of her anger and humiliation had abated, she'd dug it out and tossed it into her jewelry box. It had worked its way down into a corner, where it remained for several years, until she discovered it by accident and took it to a jeweler to have the clasp repaired.

Shannon noticed that Clint's brows were drawn together in a slight frown, as if he were trying to make up his mind about something. He stared down at her, his dark eyes holding hers. "Ah, listen, Shannon . . ." he began, with an air of having come to a decision. But his words trailed off as he realized the music had stopped. Glancing around, he saw that people were leaving the dance floor. Almost reluctantly, he released her.

Shannon expected him to escort her back to the friends she'd been with when he'd asked her to dance. Instead, with a hand on her arm, he ushered her past those friends, who were watching their every move with unabashed interest, past the party area, to a secluded corner of the backyard.

Once they were by themselves Clint reached for her hand, his strong warm grasp enveloping her slim fingers. At first they didn't talk as they strolled along hand in hand. Clint was the first to break the silence.

"I never got the chance to tell you that you looked very beautiful the night of your birthday party, and . . ." His deep voice was a rough caress. ". . . you look even more beautiful tonight."

Shannon could feel the little pulse at the base of her throat pounding, and she was relieved that the darkness hid the sudden tinge of pink that splashed across her cheeks. She had the feeling she'd slipped back into one of those girlish daydreams she used to have as a teenager. Almost afraid to say anything that might break the spell, she finally managed to murmur a brief "Thank you."

They lapsed into silence again. Clint appeared to be deep in thought. Shannon sensed he had something on his mind, and by the time he spoke she was in an agony of anticipation.

"When you told me a little while ago that you used to be 'incurably romantic' "—he sounded as if he were thinking each word over carefully—"did you mean the only reason you told me you loved me that night was because you were a fanciful teenager and we were in a romantic setting?"

Shannon's thoughts were tangled in a whirl of emotions as she weighed her reply. Had he been feeling guilty all these years because he'd dashed her hopes? She thought about laughing lightly and tossing off a casual reply, something like, *Yes, I was such a silly teenager, wasn't I?* That would let him off the hook and ease his conscience, as well as salvaging her own pride. On the other hand . . .

"I've often wondered what would have happened if I'd taken you a little more seriously," he went on.

Shannon's heart slammed against her ribs. Was he admitting that if he hadn't been involved with Valerie, he might have been inclined to look on her as more than just that "nice kid next door"?

He stopped walking and turned to face her. There was something intense in the way he looked at her. Unexpectedly, he reached out and traced a finger down the line of her jaw lightly, his gentle touch igniting a warm glow deep inside her. "When are you going back to Seattle?"

"I—I'm not sure," she replied, flustered. "In a few

weeks, I suppose—Dad's getting around almost normally again . . .''

"Can't you stay here a while longer?" His tone was low and earnest. "We need to talk—to work things out. There's a lot we need to get settled between us." He couldn't let her go away until they'd had a chance to examine their feelings. He had to know if there was anything left of that love she'd once professed to have for him.

What was he trying to say? Shannon looked up into his eyes, and what she saw there told her everything she needed to know. For several seconds she almost forgot to breathe, as she considered the implications of his request. She sensed that her entire future could depend on how she responded.

"I-I—" When she tried to reply her powers of speech failed her. She inhaled a deep draft of air into her lungs and made another attempt. "Clint—"

"That you out there, Clint?"

Shannon struggled to bring her emotions under control as Brady Murdoch's gravelly voice cut through the darkness.

"I've been looking all over for you," Brady said, coming toward them. "One of your hands just called. Seems there's some problem out at your place. I didn't get the whole story because someone else took the message, but it had something to do with that new bull you just bought."

Clint's brow furrowed into a frown. "I'd better call and see what's going on. I'll be right back."

"Hope I didn't interrupt anything," Brady said to Shannon as they watched Clint's retreating back.

"No, we—we were just . . . talking." With a feeling

of resignation, she accompanied Brady back to the party area.

Shannon felt as if she were playing a role, as she made light conversation with some of the other guests. She wondered if anyone sensed the war of emotions that raged beneath her casual demeanor. Oh, she didn't blame Clint. She'd been a rancher's daughter long enough to know how important a good bull was. If anything happened to the animal there would be no calf crop next year. And a ranch's livelihood depended on those calves. Still, it seemed as if a cruel Fate was playing a malicious joke on her, building her up to believe her dreams were at last coming true, only to dash her hopes.

"Yes, I'm working for a software company in Seattle," she said, in answer to a question one of the guests had asked her. "They're holding my job open for me—"

She felt a hand on her arm.

"You'll excuse Shannon, won't you?" Clint said to the woman she'd been talking to. Without waiting for a reply, he drew her off to one side. "Ah, listen, Shannon—I have to leave. My bull got caught in some barbed wire, and got cut up pretty bad. The vet's already been called, but I think I should be there to see what's going on. That's a pretty valuable animal, and I don't want to take any chances with him. You understand, don't you?"

"Of course," Shannon replied, summoning a smile that belied her disappointment. "I hope everything will be all right."

Clint shifted his weight from one foot to the other,

as if he couldn't quite bring himself to leave yet. ''You know what we were talking about just before Brady came along—we'll finish that conversation very soon.'' His voice was intense. ''I'll call you in a day or two.''

With that, he leaned down and kissed her very thoroughly on the lips, apparently oblivious to the curious stares of those around them. Then he was gone, leaving Shannon with the feeling that the events of the last hour or so had been nothing more than figments of her sometimes too-fertile imagination.

Chapter Eleven

Bethany regarded her father thoughtfully across the breakfast table. "Daddy, when are you and Shannon going to get married?" she asked as she finished her cereal and put the spoon down next to the bowl.

Clint took a hasty swallow of coffee to keep from choking on the bite of fried egg he'd just put in his mouth. The still-hot liquid burned his tongue and made his eyes smart. "What makes you think we're going to get married?" he asked, when he was able to speak again.

"Well, Melissa's mother and dad were at that party you went to the other night—you know, the one at Mr. and Mrs. Murdoch's—and Melissa heard her mother tell her Aunt Jennifer that you kissed Shannon—right in front of everyone." She picked up a triangle of toast and nibbled the corners. "When people kiss each other that means they're in love, doesn't it? And if people are in love they get married," she finished up, as if that settled the matter.

Clint took another sip of coffee—more cautiously this time—while he considered his reply. He wished the matter were as cut and dried as his daughter seemed to think it was. If it were left up to him he'd

133

have Shannon in front of Pastor Colton so fast she'd hardly know what was happening.

Any last, lingering doubts he might have had about his feelings for her had been dispelled. There was no longer any question in his mind. He was hopelessly, irrevocably in love with Shannon. He'd finally admitted that to himself in the wee hours of the morning as he lay staring into the darkness, unable to sleep. He wanted to spend the rest of his life with her. It was that simple.

But did she feel the same way? Although she'd admitted she'd once loved him—ten years ago—she'd been little more than a child then, too young to really know her own mind. The question was, did she love him *now?* After that interlude when they'd been locked in the tack shed together, he had to assume there was still a spark of whatever feelings she'd once had for him.

Still, she *had* been away for a number of years, a little voice in the back of his mind reminded him. She'd been living in a large city, where such matters were taken more lightly than they would be here.

Past experience had taught him to be cautious. He had no intention of baring his heart and soul until he had some idea how *she* felt. For all he knew, she might already be regretting what had happened. Granted, she'd admitted, at the Murdochs' party, that she'd once loved him—when she was sixteen. That didn't mean she was *still* in love with him, though.

He'd have to proceed slowly, cautiously, one step at a time. They'd never even had a real date. He could start by calling her and asking her to have dinner with him.

If she said yes he could take her to The Branding Iron, a steak house on the outskirts of town. Although its folksy, down-home atmosphere might not be exactly conducive to the romantic mood he hoped to create, it was the best Liberty had to offer. If they could find a relatively secluded corner booth, and if they weren't spotted by too many well-meaning acquaintances, he hoped they could have a serious talk about where their relationship was heading—or even, if there *was* a relationship.

He realized Bethany was looking at him expectantly, waiting for an answer to her question. "It's not that simple, honey," he said. "I haven't asked her yet, you know."

"Well then, *do* it," the little girl urged, as she popped the last of her toast into her mouth and wiped the crumbs from her fingers. "Melissa's mother told her Aunt Jennifer that she couldn't for the life of her see what the two of you were waiting for."

"Now, Bethany—" His words were interrupted by a loud bang, as Thelma closed a cupboard door with a good deal more force than seemed necessary. Both father and daughter glanced at the housekeeper curiously. Although her back was toward them, everything about her angular form radiated disapproval.

"Bethany, if you're finished with your breakfast, go brush your teeth," Clint said.

"But Daddy, you didn't tell me when you're going to marry Shannon."

"We'll discuss that later. When, and if, Shannon and I decide to get married, I promise you'll be the first to know. Now *scoot*."

Reluctantly, Bethany got up from the table and

started across the kitchen, dragging her feet. Just as she reached the door, she paused and turned back to her father. "Can I be a flower girl? Melissa got to be a flower girl at her Aunt Jennifer's wedding—"

"*Go.*"

With a resigned shrug she made her exit, heaving one last long, dramatic sigh on her way out. Once she was gone Clint directed his attention back to his housekeeper, who was at the counter slicing apples for a pie. "Now what's got *you* all upset?"

"What makes you think I'm upset?" Thelma asked in an elaborately casual tone.

"For starters, the way you're trying to break the cupboard doors."

With an audible sniff, Thelma whirled around, knife in hand. "Far be it from me to butt in where it's none of my business. Even though I've worked for you for so long that you and Bethany are like my own family, I wouldn't dream of trying to tell you how to manage your life."

Clint raised an eyebrow. Thelma had been a part of his life while he was growing up, whenever extra help was needed around the house, and she'd come back to take over the running of his household when he'd found himself trying to raise a child alone. In all that time he'd never known her to be reticent about expressing her opinion.

"If you *did* have something to say, what would it be?"

"Since you ask, I'd tell you it's time you woke up and smelled the coffee. I swear, I don't know why you keep poking along, wasting time. That little girl needs a mother, and *you* need a wife.'' She shook the knife at him for emphasis.

This was too much. First his daughter, and now his housekeeper. Couldn't they just leave him alone and let him handle things his own way—in his own time?

''If you don't get busy and take some positive action, that girl's going to be on her way back to Seattle,'' Thelma warned.

''Do you think I ought to ask Shannon how she feels about all this?'' Clint asked drily, ''or should I just grab her by the hair and drag her off to Pastor Colton?''

''All right, joke about it if you like. But mark my words, if you keep on stalling she's going to get tired of waiting.'' Thelma punctuated the air with her knife. ''A girl likes to know where she stands—''

''I have to get going,'' Clint said, interrupting what showed signs of turning into a lengthy lecture. ''I've got a a lot of things to do today.'' He realized he'd better make his exit before the housekeeper really got wound up. Taking a last hasty swallow of coffee, he got up from the table.

A short time later he was in his pickup heading down the long curved driveway that led to the main road, not sure exactly where he was going. After that scene in the kitchen, he'd abandoned the idea of calling Shannon. Oh, he still planned to ask her out, but with the two females in his household so interested in his social life, he doubted he'd be able to find the privacy to make a phone call from home. He was out of practice at asking women for dates, and he shrank from the thought of Bethany or Thelma overhearing his side of the conversation.

He supposed if he hung around the arena when he dropped Bethany off for drill practice this afternoon he might get a chance to have a word with Shannon. He quickly discarded that plan, however. He'd have even less opportunity to talk to her in private there than he would at home. He had a sudden mental picture of trying to ask Shannon out with the entire drill team gathered around, hanging on his every word. Scratch *that* idea.

He needed to see John about that strip of land they were irrigating. If he went over there this morning he might get a few minutes alone with Shannon. That sounded like his best bet. With an air of having come to a decision, he headed in the direction of the McCrae ranch when he reached the main road.

It would be easier to ask her out this way than over the phone, anyway. If he called, he'd have to get right to the point, but if he just happened to run into her while visiting her father, they could make light conversation while he gauged her feelings. Then, if he judged that she'd be receptive to going to dinner with him, he could slip a casual, offhanded invitation into the conversation.

He knew he was being ridiculous. He was as nervous as a teenage boy trying to gather his courage to ask a girl out for the first time. He was haunted by the fear that he may have misinterpreted the depth of Shannon's feelings for him, though.

One step at a time, he reminded himself. The first order of business was to ask her to go out with him. Over dinner they could take time to explore what was happening between them, and where they were going from there.

By the time he reached the McCrae place, he'd regained some of his usual air of unruffled self-control. He even managed a jaunty whistle. His step was firm and purposeful, and his chin was set at a determined angle as he alighted from the truck.

"Howdy, Clint," John greeted him, stepping out of the barn. "C'mon up to the house. I've got some coffee on."

As the two men walked across the backyard together, John commented, "Heard your bull got into a little trouble the other night. Everything okay?"

"I think so. He'll have several scars to show for his night's adventure though." Briefly, he described the animal's injuries. "Maybe this'll teach him to not go wandering off on his own."

"Glad to hear it wasn't any worse," John replied. "Be a shame to lose a good bull."

An insistent ringing could be heard in another part of the house as they came in the back door. "Help yourself, while I get that," John said. "You know where everything is." With that, he went off to answer the phone.

With the easy familiarity of one who was a frequent visitor there, Clint got a mug out of the cupboard and filled it from the coffeemaker on the counter. Where was Shannon? he wondered.

His question was answered a few seconds later as he heard John say, "Nope, she's not here. She and her ma went into town to do some shopping."

Clint felt a stab of disappointment. It hadn't occurred to him that Shannon might not be home, after he'd finally mustered the courage to come over and ask her out. *You idiot,* he berated himself. *Did you think she was just going to sit around waiting for you to get your act together?*

"I'll have her call you when she gets in," John went on, "but she probably won't be back until this afternoon." There was a pause, then, "Sure, I'll be glad to take a message. Just give me a minute to find a pencil and something to write on."

As Clint leaned against the counter sipping his coffee, he wondered idly who was so anxious to reach Shannon, and why, but he reminded himself it was none of his business. He tried not to listen, but he couldn't completely shut out John's voice. A shock wave ran through him as the name ". . . Paul Foster . . ." drifted out to him. Wasn't that the guy Shannon worked for—the one who sent her roses?

In spite of Clint's best intentions not to eavesdrop, the cryptic message, "All Sims's material on the Golden Door project will be ready for her as soon as she gets back . . ." drifted out to him as John repeated the information he was taking down. "The client has agreed that a few days' delay won't present any big problem. The offer's still open if she can be here by the beginning of next week . . ."

There was more, but Clint didn't want to hear it. He took his coffee cup and went out to stand on the back step. Apparently this Paul Foster was trying to lure Shannon back with promises of . . . He wasn't sure what.

"Clint, where'd you get to?" John called.

"I'm out here."

John came out to join him a few seconds later, carrying a mug of coffee. "That was that Foster guy on the phone—Shannon's boss. I'm not sure just what's going on, but it seems they need Shannon back on the job as soon as possible. Foster called last night and Shannon had a long talk with him in the study. I haven't gotten the whole story from Shannon yet, but from what I've been able to piece together, it seems there's some kind of emergency at that place where she works—Software Specialties. They want her to come back right away to finish some important project. She mentioned something about a promotion being offered to her if she can pull it off.''

Clint felt as if he'd been punched in the stomach. From what John said, Shannon was obviously planning to accept that offer.

How could he have been such a fool? He'd actually allowed himself to believe she would consider giving up her life in Seattle to make her home in a small town in the middle of nowhere. He could confront her, but what would be the point, other than to cause himself even more pain? Obviously those moments in the tack shed had meant no more to her than a brief diversion, a way to pass the time until she went back to Seattle. The beginning of a harsh, bitter laugh escaped his lips before he was able to choke it back.

John, seemingly lost in his own thoughts, glanced at him curiously. ''I'm real pleased that Shannon's career is going so well, but . . .'' He paused to take a sip of coffee. ''. . . I'd sort of hoped she'd make up her mind to not go back. I thought she might decide she'd had enough of city life and was ready to settle down here.'' His tone held a note of regret.

Clint gave a little offhanded shrug. ''Yeah, well, I guess there's not much to offer a young woman in a place like this.'' He should know that better than anyone. He winced inwardly, recalling Valerie's resentment when it had been necessary for them to leave Los Angeles and move to the ranch after his father's death. Right from the first, she'd been restless and discontented away from the bright lights and glitter of southern California.

"I don't see why it's *your* responsibility to come back here and run this place," she'd fumed. "If your mother doesn't want to run it herself, why doesn't she just sell it?"

There was no way he could even consider letting that happen. The ranch wasn't just an obligation to him. It was part of who he was. From the time he was small there had always been the awareness that someday he'd be the one running it. It had been in the family for several generations, and he looked forward to passing it on to his own children.

"Valerie, we discussed all this before we were married," he'd reminded her. "You knew we'd eventually be moving back here and I'd be taking over the ranch."

She seemed determined to wear him down with tears and temper tantrums, though, until he felt as if he were being torn in two. By then he'd had enough of city life, and working for Valerie's uncle, and the idea of returning to Los Angeles was abhorrent to him. The courses he'd taken in college had been to prepare him to manage the ranch's business affairs, not so he could spend long, boring days in a stuffy, airless office shuffling papers around.

He'd hoped, now that they had a child, Valerie would be more inclined to settle down. Motherhood only seemed to increase her discontent, though, until eventually she'd simply gone back to southern California on her own, leaving Clint and their daughter to fend for themselves.

Although Bethany had been little more than a baby at the time, she'd been old enough to miss her mother. For a long time she'd gone around like a little waif during the day, and she'd cried herself to sleep every night.

He felt a pang of regret that she'd have to go through that again, when Shannon left. Obviously, he'd been right to be concerned about her growing fondness for Shannon. At least, he consoled himself, it was a good thing he found out now where Shannon's loyalties lay, before Bethany became any more attached to her.

That period after Valerie left had been the darkest, most dismal of his entire life. It had taken him a long time to get over the bitterness and disillusionment, and he'd vowed he'd never expose himself or his daughter to that kind of misery again.

And now it seemed he'd come dangerously close to making the same mistake. From what John had just told him, Shannon was no more interested in settling down here than Valerie had been. He reminded himself he was fortunate to have found this out now, before he let himself in for more heartache.

That thought failed to give him any comfort, though.

Chapter Twelve

"You're looking great," Shannon called out from her position in the center of the ring. "Don't forget to hold those flags up straight. The judges notice things like that." She had to raise her voice to be heard over the low, thunderlike rumble in the distance. "Trish, remember to keep your elbows in."

She was proud of their progress. She hoped they wouldn't have too much trouble finding someone to fill in as advisor while she was in Seattle. She almost felt as if she were deserting them, even though she had only agreed to take on the job in the first place until someone permanent could be found. Since nobody else had come forward to take over the position, it seemed it was hers for as long as she was here.

Anyway, if everything went well she wouldn't be gone more than a few weeks. She hadn't mentioned to the team members that she was leaving. She wanted to tell Clint first, before he heard it from someone else, so she could make sure he understood it was only temporary. She'd hoped to see him when he brought Bethany to practice, so she could let him know she had something important to talk to him about. Somehow she'd missed him, though. She'd been busy writing out some instructions for whoever would take her place while she was away, and when she'd looked up Clint had already dropped Bethany off and left.

And she had to let her parents know what her plans were. They were already aware that Paul wanted her to come back to work right away, but she hadn't had a chance to explain the whole situation to them.

Glancing at her watch she saw, with relief, that it was almost time for the session to end. Despite the best efforts of the kids, it hadn't been a good day to practice. Hank Archer, whose ranch adjoined the property the arena was on, had been blasting stumps down on his south pasture all afternoon. The periodic bursts of noise were making the horses skittish and edgy. It was unnerving, rather like being in the middle of a battle zone.

Clint would be coming to pick up Bethany before long. Shannon's pulse quickened in anticipation of seeing him again. Since the Murdochs' party two days ago, he had been in her thoughts constantly.

In her mind, she'd replayed every detail of the time she'd spent with him at the party, from the minute he'd swept her onto the dance floor until he'd kissed her good-bye—with a good many of the Murdochs' guests looking on.

What would have happened if he hadn't had to leave so suddenly? she wondered. He'd asked her to not go back to Seattle for a while. "There's a lot we need to get settled," he'd said. Had he been on the verge of telling her he loved her and wanted her to stay here?

Ever since the party she'd been letting her mind play "what if" with the idea of giving up her life in

Seattle, and all that went with it—her job, her apartment, her friends. What if she just didn't go back at all? She had no doubt she could find a job where she could utilize her skills in Liberty or one of the nearby towns. After all, all but the very smallest businesses relied on computers these days. And the friend who was subletting her furnished apartment had already expressed a desire to take over her lease. She was sure she could prevail on that same friend to pack up her clothes and personal belongings.

So far, though, she'd only been *toying* with the idea of staying here. She'd expected to have another week or two, at least, in which to make up her mind—until that troubling phone call she'd gotten from Paul last night had forced her hand.

Briefly, Paul had explained that Earl Sims, who had been with him ever since he'd started his company, had suffered a sudden heart attack and was in the hospital.

Shannon's heart had gone out to the quiet-spoken, middle-aged man. "I'm so sorry to hear that!" she'd exclaimed. "Is he going to be all right?"

"He's coming along fine," Paul assured her. "I just came from visiting him. There's a problem, though. As you know, Earl was right in the middle of putting together that program for the Golden Door," he went on, referring to a restaurant chain in western Washington. "Since you've worked with him on it, I was hoping I could persuade you to come back here and finish it."

"But after all the time Earl's put into it, he'll want to see it through himself, won't he?" Although she was flattered that Paul had so much confidence in her, it seemed a breach of professional courtesy to step in and take over someone else's project.

"Earl won't be coming back," Paul said after a brief pause. "He's decided to take an early retirement. He says this heart attack made him realize how short life is, and he wants to give himself more time to fish and play golf, and to get to know his grandchildren better."

A multitude of thoughts ran through Shannon's mind as she considered the implications of this new development.

"I could turn the project over to another employee," Paul went on, "but anyone else would have to start from scratch and that would take too long. The client needs it as soon as possible. If we can't provide it they'll have to go to another company. The Golden Door is one of our biggest accounts, you know, and I'd hate to lose their business. I realize I told you to stay there as long as you feel you're needed, but I'm really counting on you to come through for me."

When he put it that way she didn't see how she could refuse. Paul had been more than just her employer, he was a good friend. She owed it to him to help him out on this. Besides, in all honesty, if she intended to go back at all, she could no longer use her father's accident as an excuse for delaying her return. His cast would be coming off any day, and, except for a slight limp, he was getting around as well as he ever had.

"And Shannon," Paul went on, "I'd like you to take over Earl's old job when you come back."

She knew the promotion wasn't being offered just as a bribe. She'd worked hard, and had earned it. At one time she'd have been elated to have been given this opportunity to prove her worth to the company. But now, having a successful career paled in comparison to what she would be giving up. She hesitated, weighing her reply carefully.

"Shannon, are you still there?"

"Yes, I'm here, Paul. I'll come back long enough to finish up this project, but I don't want the promotion. I—I'm planning on turning in my resignation. I've decided to stay here in Liberty."

She hadn't meant to blurt it out that way. She hadn't even made up her mind yet—at least not consciously. Once the words were out, though, she was surprised at how relieved she felt.

During the silence that followed she could picture the look in Paul's blue eyes, the expression of puzzled concern that would mar his pleasant features.

It wasn't just her job she was turning her back on, of course. There were other, more subtle factors involved.

Paul had made it clear that he'd like to be the man in her life. She knew he'd sensed that she had a reason for holding him at arm's length, that she had some unfinished business to put behind her. He hadn't rushed her in this, but had stood by patiently, ready to offer support if it was needed. She could tell, though, he was hoping that when she returned she'd be ready for more than the casual relationship she'd always been careful to maintain between them. It was nothing against Paul, of course. He was her dear friend. It was just that nobody ever lived up to the image she had of Clint.

She'd had some idea, when she returned home, that

once she saw Clint again she'd be able to get over this habit of comparing every man she met to him. She needed to accept the fact that the future with him she'd fantasized about as a teenager was just that, a fantasy. It was time to put these silly, childish daydreams out of her mind and get on with her life. And getting on with her life meant allowing herself to at least consider falling in love with someone else.

All that was before the events of the last few days, though, before Clint had asked, "Can't you stay here a while longer?" Before he'd said, "We need to talk—to work things out . . . there's a lot we need to get settled."

She *couldn't* leave now—not until she found out just what he'd meant. If she did she'd spend the rest of her life wondering if she had made a mistake . . .

Paul's voice had brought her back to the matter at hand. "You're staying there? I don't understand."

She didn't blame him for being puzzled. She couldn't tell him the real reason for her decision. "I— I guess being back has made me realize this is where I belong."

"You can't bury yourself way out there," he protested. "Not when you have such a promising future."

"Montana is my home," she reminded him. "And I've been away too long."

The conversation had ended on an uncertain note. She'd promised to come back long enough to finish up the Golden Door account, if he could give her just a few more days.

She was hoping it wouldn't be necessary for her to leave until after the Founders Day rodeo, which was coming up this weekend. Although it was just a small, local affair, it was something she'd been looking forward to. She and her parents had taken part in it for as long as she could remember. She'd won her first ribbon in barrel-racing at that very rodeo, and her father had been chairman of the rodeo committee for the past several years.

Besides, the drill team would be putting on an exhibition between events, as well as participating in the Grand Entry Parade. She'd be letting them down if she left before the rodeo.

Paul had agreed to talk to the representatives from the Golden Door to see if they could wait that long. Shannon sensed that he was hoping once she got back to Seattle she'd have a change of heart about giving up her job.

Apparently he'd been able to square things with the Golden Door people. When she'd arrived home from shopping this afternoon she found his latest message next to the telephone. She hadn't been able to return the call though, since she had to get to drill practice and she was already running late. Her reply hadn't changed from what she'd told him last night, anyway. As soon as the Golden Door project was finished she'd be on her way back to Montana—and to Clint. A tingle of excitement ran through her . . .

She wondered what Clint's reaction would be when she told him of her decision to remain here. She allowed her imagination to conjure up a picture of him tenderly pulling her into his arms and whispering, in a voice husky with emotion, that he didn't ever want them to be separated again . . .

She was enjoying the scenario—until a sudden loud

crack jolted her back to reality. She sighed. Hank Archer was still at it.

There was time enough for daydreaming about Clint later, anyway. Right now there were other matters to attend to.

"Let's run through the whole routine one last time," she called out briskly to the team members. *Might as well give it up for today,* she thought, as several more loud reports, in rapid succession, shattered the air. After a brief interval of relative quiet, she'd dared hope Hank might have abandoned the attack on his stumps. Apparently he'd only been taking a coffee break, though, and was now returning to the battle with a renewed vigor.

While she waited for the riders to take their places she noticed a movement, through the wide opening at one end of the arena. As if thinking about Clint had conjured up his presence, she spotted his pickup and horse trailer pulling into the parking lot.

As she watched him get out of the truck and saunter towards the arena she couldn't help noticing how the late-afternoon sun behind him silhouetted his slim, muscular figure. The faded denim jeans he wore emphasized his lean grace in a way that made her feel weak inside, as if her bones were melting . . .

This would never do. Deliberately, she forced her gaze back to the team. They were sitting as still as statues, waiting for her signal. At her nod, twenty-four riders nudged their horses into action.

As they approached the far end of the arena Shannon could see Clint standing just outside. Why wasn't he coming in? she wondered, with a little stab of disappointment. After his parting words the night of the party, she'd expected him to be as eager to see her again as she was to see him. Most likely, though, he didn't want to interrupt her practice session. Maybe that was just as well, anyway. These kids were pretty perceptive, and they were bound to notice the electricity flowing between the two of them. She sensed that he'd prefer to keep their relationship as private as possible—at least until they had made some kind of commitment to each other. Their slow-moving romance had already become a matter for too much public conjecture.

By now the riders had reached the point in their routine where they had paired off and were circling the ring in twos. She surveyed them with a critical eye, alert for any flaws in their performance. When her glance came to Bethany, she smiled at the look of intense concentration on the little girl's face.

Her attention shifted to Cody, riding next to Bethany. The youngest member of the team, he wasn't quite as accomplished a rider as some of the others, and sometimes needed a little extra instruction. Right now his horse, Pete, was starting to pull ahead.

"Cody," she called out, "keep in step—"

Her words were drowned out by a sudden explosion that thundered through the arena with such force that the ground shook. Caught off guard, Shannon was almost jolted out of her saddle by the impact. Her heart began pounding like a trip-hammer as a jolt of adrenaline spread through her system. *Hank must have run across a particularly stubborn stump,* she thought wryly, as the reverberations died away.

Feeling a nervous shudder run through her horse, she automatically tightened her hold on the reins.

"There, there," she murmured in low, comforting tones, at the same time scanning the group of riders to make sure everyone was all right. Although several of them had let out startled exclamations and somebody had dropped a flag, nobody seemed to have panicked. She noted that Cody was having a problem calming Pete, though. The little gelding was rolling its eyes in fright and tossing its head.

"Cody, hold the reins the way I showed you," she called, giving her own horse a nudge so she could come to his aid. At the same time, out of the corner of her eye, she saw Clint running into the arena. Evidently, he'd been watching the proceedings from his vantage point just outside the entrance.

Before she was halfway across the ring, Pete shied to one side, forcing Bethany's horse over toward the wooden railing. Bethany winced slightly as her arm scraped against the rough planking.

Shannon reached the two riders seconds before Clint did. By that time Cody had regained control of the skittish animal, and Bethany was rubbing her arm. The other riders were turning in their saddles as they craned to see what was happening.

"Everything's okay," Shannon assured them as she dismounted. "Why don't we call it a day? I'll let you know when the next practice will be."

Almost reluctantly, as if they'd sensed some kind of hidden undercurrent in the air and were curious to see what was going to take place next, the team members began to leave. While the arena was emptying, Shannon turned her attention back to the two children. "Are either of you hurt?" she asked.

Cody shook his head.

"Bethany? I'd better have a look at that arm."

"It's okay. It just got scraped a little." She held the limb out for Shannon's inspection.

Clint shouldered past Shannon. "Let me see." Frowning, he examined his daughter's arm carefully, although the only sign of any injury was a slight reddening on the skin.

"I said it's *all right,* Daddy," Bethany insisted. She seemed embarrassed at having so much fuss made over nothing. "Honest, it's not even a little bit sore."

Finally, apparently satisfied that she was unhurt, Clint said, "Why don't you take Sandy out to the trailer? I'll be along in a minute or two. And Cody, you'd better get going too." Although he didn't add, *Before you cause any more trouble,* there was little doubt that was what he was thinking.

As Cody and Bethany left the arena Clint whirled to face Shannon, an expression in his dark eyes that she didn't recognize. She felt a sharp tingle of apprehension.

When the two children were out of earshot, Clint said accusingly, "This is all your fault, you know." Although his tone was low and controlled, the hostility in his voice was so strong that Shannon took an involuntary step backward, her mouth dropping open in shocked surprise.

"If you'd listened to me, this wouldn't have happened," he went on.

Shannon couldn't have been more stunned if he'd struck her. "Wh-what—"

"You know what I'm talking about. I told you Bethany wasn't old enough to be in drill team. She doesn't have enough experience. You should have backed me up, instead of encouraging her.''

''But—but experience had nothing to do with what took place,'' she said, through lips that felt stiff. ''It could have happened to anyone. Anyway, she wasn't hurt.''

''But she could have been. What if she'd been thrown and trampled?'' Clint demanded. ''Or crushed up against that railing? If Bethany were *your* daughter, maybe you'd be a little more concerned about what happens to her.''

Although Shannon was beginning to sense that this was about something more than a minor mishap, she could feel her anger rising. Whatever had happened to make him overreact this way, he had no right to take it out on her. How dare he insinuate that Bethany's safety and well-being were of little importance to her?

She was completely baffled by his attitude. Surely he understood that minor scrapes and bruises—and sometimes worse—were a part of childhood. She recalled the time Bethany had appeared at drill practice sporting an Ace bandage around her wrist. ''I was practicing barrel-racing in the field behind our barn,'' the little girl had explained, with a nonchalant shrug, ''and I got too close to the barrel.'' Another time she'd shown up with a noticeable limp, and had admitted to falling out of a tree. In each instance, Clint—in spite of his overprotectiveness where Bethany was concerned—had seemed to accept the fact that children did occasionally get hurt. Why was he being so inconsistent now?

''Clint, what's gotten into you?'' she demanded, in

a burst of righteous indignation. ''Why are you making such a big deal out of a minor incident?''

''Minor incident!'' Clint echoed. ''She could have been seriously injured. I should have realized,'' he went on, as if her words confirmed his suspicions, ''you don't really care a thing about Bethany. Or about me!'' With that, he turned and strode off.

This can't be happening, Shannon thought, a shock wave rolling over her. ''Clint, wait—'' she called after him, when she could find her voice. She hardly dared breathe as he slowed down almost imperceptibly. For just a second she was sure he was going to come back so they could discuss this like rational people. But then he picked up his pace.

Tears of anger and frustration stung her eyes as she stared after his retreating form. What on earth had gotten into him? And what had he meant by that last remark, *''You don't really care a thing about Bethany—or about me''*?

She loved Bethany very much, and would never have knowingly exposed the child to any harm. And as for her feelings toward Clint—surely he must know how much she loved him.

She waited until she was sure the parking lot was empty and everyone had gone home before she ventured outside the arena. She couldn't face anyone while this chaotic mixture of hurt and anger seethed inside her.

''You got a call from Paul Foster,'' John said. ''Did you find the message I left by the phone?''

''Yes, I saw it.'' In the hours since she'd returned from drill practice Shannon had managed to regain enough control over her shattered emotions that she could trust her voice to not waver when she spoke. She thought she sounded quite normal now. To listen to her, nobody would guess that a heavy lump of misery had settled like a rock in her midsection. "What time did he call?"

"Sometime this morning. Early, I guess—right after Clint got here."

At this bit of information, a multitude of thoughts, all jumbled together, raced through her mind. "Oh." Her tone was elaborately casual. "Clint came by this morning?"

John nodded. "We were just coming in to have some coffee when the phone rang."

So Clint had been in the house while her father was taking down the message. She could imagine how it must have sounded to him. She recalled phrases from the note: ... *as soon as you can get back... if you can be here by the beginning of next week...* And John might even have mentioned to Clint, like the proud father he was, that she was up for a promotion when she returned to work. If Clint thought she was going back to Seattle for good, that would account for his odd behavior this afternoon.

But it didn't excuse it.

If he loved her he would have waited to hear her side of the story before immediately jumping to a wrong conclusion. In which case, there wasn't much point in hanging around, was there? Now that his feelings for her had been made so painfully clear, it would be downright masochistic to stay here, where she would be constantly reminded that he'd once again rejected the love she offered him.

John glanced at her closely. ''You feelin' all right, girl?''

''What? Oh—yes. I was just thinking I'd better return Paul's call and let him know when I'll be arriving.'' She was proud of the way she was controlling her voice. She even managed a smile. ''This promotion I've been offered is a terrific opportunity. I'd be foolish not to accept it.''

Chapter Thirteen

The crowd in the bleachers stood in respectful silence during the playing of the national anthem. As the last notes faded away, the participants in the Grand Entry Parade—including contestants, local officials, the drill team, clowns, and pickup men—began to file out of the arena.

After a brief crackle of static the announcer's drawl floated out over the loudspeaker. "Are y'all ready for a good time?"

The spectators in the bleachers responded with applause and cheers.

"All right, then—*let's rodeo!*"

With that, the annual Liberty Founders Day Rodeo was under way.

"Where's Dad?" Shannon asked her mother as she took her seat.

"Oh, he's around someplace. I'll be lucky to get a glimpse of him."

Shannon smiled understandingly. She knew John would be all over the place, doing his best to see that things moved along on schedule. And they usually did, which was why the rodeo committee appointed him chairman year after year. He had been here since early this morning, overseeing every detail, from the location of portable rest rooms to the order in which events were to take place.

Shannon savored the sensations around her. The pungent aroma of hot dogs and mustard, mingled with the smell of horses and leather; the bawl of calves in the holding pens; the American flag and colorful pennants that fluttered in the light breeze; even the feel of the rough wooden seats and the gritty taste of the dust stirred up by the riders in the arena were achingly familiar.

She wanted to preserve every single memory to take with her when she returned to Seattle. She realized she was facing some pretty bleak days ahead, and it was comforting to know she would at least have these recollections to sustain her through the lonely times.

Her bags were packed, her airplane reservations made for a late afternoon flight. Once the rodeo was over she'd just have time to freshen up and change from her jeans into something more suitable for travel, before being driven to the small feeder airport in the next town.

A wave of premature homesickness rose up in her at the thought of all she was leaving behind—her parents, Bethany, the drill team . . .   . . . Clint.

It seemed some kind of cruel paradox that the person who was the cause of her going away was the one she was going to miss the most. For a brief time he'd begun to put aside the mistrust and doubts that had been the legacy of his former marriage, to acknowledge that he cared for her. But then those same doubts had reappeared at the first suspicion that she might have the same feelings as Valerie about ranch life.

She knew she could go to him and force him to listen to the truth. Once he heard the whole story he'd have to realize how wrong he'd been. What was the point, though? If he had so little faith in her that he immediately jumped to the wrong conclusion, did they really have any chance for a future together?

No, it was better to break things off cleanly, to return to Seattle and try to put it all behind her. Maybe, in time, she could even forget Clint Gallagher and fall in love with someone else, she told herself. Deep inside, however, she knew it would be easier for her to forget just about anything else in the world . . .

"Shannon?"

"What—?" She realized her mother had asked her something and was waiting for an answer.

"I said I'm going to the refreshment stand for a hot dog. Do you want me to bring you one?"

"Oh." She forced her attention back to the present. "Ah—sure. That sounds good."

As Maureen left, Shannon tried to focus on the activity in the arena. Despite her best efforts, however, images of Clint once again invaded her thoughts, memories of being held in that strong, muscular embrace, of his lips on hers . . .

With a real effort of will, she pushed those images away. She wasn't sure just how much time had elapsed while she'd been preoccupied with her thoughts, but the bareback bronc riding seemed to be well under way. She glanced down just as the horn sounded, signaling the end of a ride. At once the pickup men went into action. While one of them assisted the cowboy in dismounting, the other reached over and deftly unbuckled the bronc's flank strap. As the strap dropped away the bronc immediately became docile, and allowed himself to be herded back to the pens.

"Mighty fine ride," the announcer congratulated the rider over the loudspeaker.

The cowboy flashed the crowd a cocky grin as he retrieved his hat from the ground and slapped it against his leg to remove the dust from it. He acknowledged the applause by raising his clasped hands over his head in a gesture of victory.

At that moment Maureen returned with two hot dogs. The one she handed to Shannon was slathered with ketchup and mustard. "I hope you still like them this way."

"It's perfect," Shannon replied after the first bite. "Nothing ever tastes as good as hot dogs at the rodeo. I'm going to miss these."

"You don't *have* to leave," Maureen said, obviously unwilling to pass up any opportunity to try to talk her daughter into changing her plans.

Shannon knew her mother meant well, but she'd hoped they wouldn't have to rehash the subject. "Mom, we've been over all this. I can't back out now. I promised Paul. He's depending on me."

"Why couldn't you return to Seattle just long enough to finish that project that's so important? Then you could come back home. You know you could easily find work around here."

"It's not that simple. There are . . . a lot of factors involved."

"I was kind of hoping something might develop between you and Clint . . ." Maureen began wistfully. Her words trailed off when she caught her daughter's look, which said, very clearly, that the matter was closed.

Still, Shannon had no doubt that her mother would feel compelled to make one last attempt. She was relieved at the announcement that came over the speaker just then.

"Folks, I'm mighty proud to introduce Liberty's own junior mounted drill team, the Silver Spurs. These kids have worked hard to perfect their skills, and have been competing—and winning—all over the state, and now they're here to put on an exhibition for us. Let's give 'em a real big hand."

Shannon could see the drill team members lined up just outside the arena. She fought back a vague feeling that she was shirking her duty, that she ought to be down there with them, making sure their costumes were in order, giving last-minute instructions and encouragement.

She had to remind herself that the team was no longer her responsibility, that she had passed on the torch, so to speak. After the word had gone out that she was returning to her job in Seattle and a new advisor was needed, the older brother of one of the kids had agreed to take over the position.

A burst of stirring march music filled the air as the riders entered the arena, pennants flying, spurs gleaming in the sunlight. Watching them go through their maneuvers, Shannon couldn't contain a thrill of pride. When they finished an almost flawless performance by lining up in a row, facing the reviewers' stand, there was a spontaneous burst of applause from the spectators.

As they sat astride their horses, still as statues, pennants held high, the team leader glanced up into the stands at Shannon. They made eye contact, and Shannon gave him a little thumbs-up sign of approval. He acknowledged this with a brief nod, before looking straight ahead.

A lump rose in Shannon's throat and she had to blink back the sudden tears that stung her eyelids.

Later on, after the team members had had time to change clothes and cool down their horses, she'd seek out Bethany and let her know she was leaving. She wasn't looking forward to it. The little girl with the serious dark eyes had become very special to her, and saying good-bye to her wasn't going to be easy.

The rest of the rodeo events seemed to fly by, the calf-roping, the barrel-racing, the steer-wrestling. Interspersed among the more serious competitions were several ''just for fun'' contests, such as wild cow milking and goat tying.

In no time the rodeo would be over and it would be time for her to leave for the airport. She suppressed the stab of regret that shot through her by telling herself she'd be much better off in Seattle, where she could put Clint completely out of her mind and devote herself to her career. After all, it was pointless to keep exposing her poor, battered emotions to this kind of hurt.

The memory of his stern countenance and his icy tone when he'd accused her of not caring about him or Bethany brought a prickle of tears to her eyes. *Don't think about it,* she told herself. She made a determined effort to pay attention to the rodeo.

It was time for the final and most dangerous event of the day.

* * *

Clint made his preparations as he waited for the bull-riding event to be announced. After examining his bull rope, he rubbed resin on it. He rolled up his sleeve and wrapped protective tape around his hand and arm. He checked his spurs to make sure they would pass inspection.

He still wasn't sure why he was doing this. True, he'd participated in rodeo events—the riskier the better—ever since his high school days, but in the past few years he was finding that such pursuits had lost their appeal for him. He was getting too old for that sort of thing, he'd told himself. It was time he settled down.

So why was he now getting ready to climb onto the back of a two-thousand-pound beast that would just as soon gore him to death as look at him?

His thoughts went back to this morning when he'd run into John while delivering Bethany's horse to the rodeo grounds. As they stood outside the small trailer that served as the rodeo office, making small talk, John commented, "I hope everything goes on schedule today, and this thing doesn't run overtime."

Clint had raised an eyebrow questioningly. "Don't tell me you're 'all rodeoed out.' I've never known you to want to leave a rodeo until the last calf's been roped and the last steer's been wrestled."

"It's not that. We have to take Shannon to the airport over in Winchester." There was a regretful note in his voice. "Her plane leaves at six o'clock."

The pain came out of the blue, exploding inside him with numbing force. Until that moment he'd almost succeeded in convincing himself it didn't matter that

Shannon was leaving, that she was going out of his life for good.

But he hadn't expected it to hurt so much.

For a little while he'd allowed himself to believe that he might be granted a second chance at finding happiness, that Shannon was different from Valerie, and would be happy living on his ranch, being his wife and Bethany's mother.

At the Murdochs' party he'd tried to make his feelings clear. Granted, he'd been a little vague about exactly what his intentions were, but then, he wasn't in the habit of rushing into things. If she was planning on going back to Seattle so soon, she should have told him then, instead of letting him think—

"Somethin' wrong, Clint?"

He realized John was looking at him curiously. He deliberately made his expression a casual mask. "I, ah, hope she has a good trip," he got out. He shifted his weight from one foot to the other. "Well, I'd better not keep you from your duties. I know you've got a lot to do before the rodeo starts."

After John was gone, Clint stood in front of the rodeo office and drew in several deep breaths, trying to ease the wrenching pain that gnawed at his insides, and the nerves that were clenched so tightly he felt like a coiled spring . . .

"How's it goin', Gallagher?" A hearty voice cut into his thoughts.

He looked up to see Skip Tabor and Marty Lovell, a couple of hands from the Lazy K, approaching.

Rocking back on his heels, Marty studied him. "You look about as unhappy as a calf that's lost his ma," he observed.

"Woman trouble; I recognize the signs," Skip put in, with a knowing grin. "I got just the cure for that. Me 'n' Marty are goin' in to sign up for the bull-riding. Nothing like tanglin' with one of them critters to take your mind off whatever's botherin' you."

The tall, lanky cowhand threw an arm over Clint's shoulder in a comradely way and, laughing, the two men drew him along toward the office. He knew he should protest, but something stopped him. Maybe this was just what he needed. Maybe doing something reckless and wild was the only thing that was going to ease the painful knot of tension inside him.

The next thing he knew he was in front of the secretary's desk, signing up for the bull-riding event. Even as he was paying his entry fee, he knew what he was doing was foolish, even a little childish. Why had he let those two jokers talk him into this? he wondered.

Anyway, it was too late to back out now, he told himself as he heard his number called. He picked up his gear and headed for the bucking chutes.

"Looks like you drew a mean one," the wrangler commented, nodding toward the animal in the chute.

That was a masterpiece of understatement, Clint thought, eyeing the massive beast, which glared back at him defiantly. He doubted if he'd ever seen a more ornery-looking critter than this ton or so of muscle, bone, and pure meanness.

"His name's Sledgehammer," the wrangler offered.

That sounded fitting. The brute looked as if his sole aim in life was to do serious bodily harm to the puny mortal who had the audacity to think he could ride him.

Good, Clint thought. In his present mood he welcomed the challenge. Except for being a one-handed ride, there were no other rules in bull-riding exept to keep from being thrown. It would take all his powers of concentration just to stay astride the animal for the required eight seconds—which could seem like an eternity.

One of the chute men assisted Clint as he wrapped his bull rope around the animal. This done, he climbed over the top rail of the chute and gingerly eased himself onto Sledgehammer's back. So far, so good. He ran his gloved hand through the handhold. As he pulled the loose end of the rope up tight he felt a gathering of force under him, as if the bull were summoning all its energy for the upcoming confrontation of strength, skill, and sheer stubbornness.

He glanced out into the arena, at the clowns who were amusing the crowd with their baggy-pants antics. He knew their purpose wasn't merely to entertain, however. Once the ride was over they would call forth every iota of their skill, even risking injury themselves, to distract the bull's attention long enough for him to get to safety.

Giving a nod to the gate tender, he blocked everything from his mind except keeping this ill-tempered brute from getting the best of him.

Shannon was just returning from the refreshment stand, a soft drink in each hand, when she heard Clint's name announced. "Did you know Clint was entered in the bull-riding event?" she asked her mother.

"No, I don't believe I heard it mentioned," Maureen replied, accepting one of the drinks Shannon held out to her. ''Why?''

''I, ah, was just a little surprised, that's all. I didn't think he . . .'' Her words trailed off as the gate jerked open and the bull exploded out of the chute like a keg of dynamite. Clint, on the animal's back, was clinging to the bull rope with one hand, while his other arm was held out to one side for balance.

With a furious bellow, the bull began to spin. The crowd yelled its encouragement as Clint struggled to stay astride the wildly gyrating beast.

''Hang in there, cowboy!''

''Stick with 'im, Clint—you can do it!''

Changing his tactics, the bull ducked his head and kicked his heels into the air in his efforts to rid himself of the creature on his back. When that didn't accomplish his purpose, he wheeled suddenly to the right. There was a gasp from the spectators as Clint struggled to maintain his tenuous balance. In apparent defiance of all the laws of gravity and physics, he managed to right himself at the last possible second.

Shannon went almost weak with relief when the horn brayed just then. She knew, however, as did the rest of the spectators, that even though Clint had stayed on for the required time, he wasn't necessarily out of danger yet. It had often been said of bull-riding that the ''git off'' was sometimes more risky than the ''staying on.''

At the sound of the horn Clint released his grip on the rope and slid his gloved hand out of the handhold. In that split second when a little corner of his attention wasn't focused on staying astride the animal, Sledgehammer gave a sudden sideways buck. The unexpected maneuver apparently caught him with his guard down. Shannon drew in her breath sharply as he went flying off to one side.

Although he was instinctively rolling out of the way of the bull's hooves almost before he hit the ground, Clint wasn't quite quick enough to avoid a glancing blow to his forehead.

Simultaneously, the rodeo clowns were running forward, to divert the animal's attention. The bull shook his head angrily and pawed the ground several times, before allowing himself to be distracted by the shouting and waving of the two clowns.

While other rodeo personnel rushed in to assist in chasing the animal back to the pens, the crowd turned its attention back to the fallen hero. A wave of applause began as Clint started to rise. It died away, and a hush settled over the arena, when he fell back to the ground, eyes closed.

"Uh-oh, folks," the announcer said, as two blue-uniformed medical technicians hurried into the arena, one of them carrying an orange case. Although his voice was calm and steady, as if to not alarm the crowd, he couldn't keep an undertone of worry from it. "It looks as if there may be a problem down there."

While all this was taking place Shannon had sat frozen, too stunned to move a muscle. Suddenly she was ten years old again, peeking around a corner of the barn. Her heart leapt into her throat as she relived all the sensations she'd felt when Clint had been thrown while riding one of his father's unbroken horses.

All at once she was galvanized into action by the sight of Clint lying there so white and still, a trickle of blood seeping from the welt on his forehead. Almost without realizing what she was doing, she jumped up from her seat. As she did so a multitude of thoughts were running through her mind. And uppermost among those thoughts was the realization of how empty and bleak her life would be if anything happened to Clint.

"Shannon, where are you—" her mother began.

But Shannon was already making her way down the bleachers. When she reached ground level she squeezed through an opening in the fence that separated the spectators from the arena.

"Hey, you can't go out there." One of the arena men reached out to detain her. Brushing his hand aside, she ran towards Clint.

She reached him a second or two after the medical technicians, who were already kneeling next to him, taking items out of their equipment case. An icy fear twisted around her heart as she sank to her knees beside him. "Clint?" Her voice came out sounding thin and wavery.

Clint's eyelids flickered several times before his eyes fastened on her.

He felt like he'd been hit with a sledgehammer. *Sledgehammer*. That was it. The last thing he remembered was hearing the horn, and wondering how he was going to get off that blasted bull. What in the world had ever possessed him to do something as loco as entering the bull-riding event, anyway? He must have been crazy.

Then it all came back to him in a rush. Shannon was returning to Seattle—her plane would be leaving in less than an hour, in fact. And like a complete idiot, he'd decided the only way to rid himself of the hurt that was eating away at him was to do something wild and reckless.

But if she was leaving so soon, why was she here, kneeling beside him, her face a mask of concern? Maybe he was hallucinating. He tried to raise his head but the slight movement sent splinters of pain through his skull.

"Wh—what are you doing here?" It hurt even to talk. And it didn't help that one of the medical technicians, the short, stocky one, was shining a light in his eye. Clint tried to wave him away, but he couldn't seem to summon the strength to put any real authority into the gesture.

"Where did you think I'd be when the man I love is lying here injured?"

The man she loved. He *had* to be hallucinating. "You'd better go," he murmured weakly. "You'll miss your plane—Do you *have* to do that!" he barked at the technician, who was now peering into his other eye with the penlight. He immediately regretted the forcefulness of his words, as the sound of his voice reverberated through his head, making it ache even worse.

Apparently satisfied with what he saw, the technician snapped the light off. Moving back a step or two, he conferred with his colleague in an undertone.

"Why are you in such a hurry to get rid of me?" Shannon demanded.

So now she was going to lay all the blame on *him*. In spite of the pounding in his head, he felt compelled to set the record straight. "Don't forget, it was—" He winced, then lowered his voice. "It was your idea to go back to Seattle. You didn't care enough about me or about Bethany to want to stay here.''

''You idiot. If you hadn't gotten in such a huff you'd have taken the time to find out that I wasn't planning to go away for good. I was only going to be in Seattle long enough to finish a project. Then I was coming right back.''

During this exchange the other technician, a lanky redhead, was wrapping a blood pressure cuff around Clint's arm. His face was an impassive mask, as if his only concern was determining the condition of his patient.

''Sure. That's why your boss is giving you a promotion.'' There was a touch of sarcasm, mingled with resignation, in his voice. What was the point in rehashing the matter, since she'd already made up her mind?

''Sometimes I don't think you have the brains God gave green apples,'' Shannon said hotly. ''You'd have known I was coming back if you'd taken the trouble to *ask*. Or if you'd *trusted* me. But no, you had to get all macho and stubborn. The only reason I changed my plans and decided to stay in Seattle was because you made it pretty clear that you *wanted* me to leave.''

Clint couldn't come up with anything in his defense. What Shannon said was true. He'd practically driven her away. Anyway, all this arguing was making his headache worse. And these two guys who kept fussing over him weren't helping the situation. Letting his breath out, he closed his eyes slowly, but they flew open again at Shannon's cry of alarm. He saw that all the color had drained from her face.

"Y-you scared me," she stammered. "I thought you—"

He shrugged, and managed a shaky version of his old cocky grin. "I'm tough as an old turkey buzzard. It'd take a lot more than getting kicked in the head by a bull to do me in."

"How can you make light of something like this?" Shannon scolded, a burst of anger beginning to replace some of her fright. "And what were you doing riding a bull, anyway? Of all the stupid things to do! You could have been killed!"

By now a small crowd had gathered—the wranglers, clowns, chute men, and other arena personnel— and had formed a loose circle around Clint, Shannon, and the two technicians. Now that it was apparent that Clint's injuries weren't life-threatening, they were watching the proceedings with interest.

Shannon was aware of the announcer's words. "Folks, I can't quite make out what's going on down there, but it appears that Clint is conscious and able to talk. At least, he seems to be carrying on a conversation with the young lady at his side. It looks like, ah—" He paused to take a closer look. "Yes, I believe it's Shannon McCrae."

The redhaired technician was trying to fit a collar or brace of some sort around Clint's neck, but Clint waved him away irritably. With difficulty, he turned onto his side. The technician put out a hand to restrain him, but Clint stopped him with a stony glare. He hoisted himself up on one elbow, his head resting on his hand.

"Would you have cared?" he asked. "If I'd been killed, I mean."

"Would I have cared?" Shannon echoed. "Of course I'd—" She became aware that they had an audience. "Yes, I'd care," she finished softly.

"But you're still going back to Seattle." The way he said it was a cross between a statement and a question, as if he were almost afraid to let himself believe she might be persuaded to change her mind.

"As I recollect," the announcer went on, "these two caused quite a stir when they showed up at the Ranchers' Association dinner together." The note of concern had left his voice and now he sounded as casual and folksy as if he were passing the time with his cronies down at Jake Ledbetter's hardware store. "They were also what I believe is considered, in some circles, to be a 'hot item,' at Viv and Brady Murdoch's anniversary shindig . . ."

As the announcer's words began to penetrate, something in Shannon snapped. She'd had just about enough of all this game-playing and pussyfooting around. Apparently everyone else in town considered her and Clint to be a couple. If he was too hardheaded and too stubborn to realize they belonged together, she was going to have to take matters into her own hands.

Squaring her shoulders and lifting her chin a fraction of an inch, she fixed Clint with a determined look. "You might as well know, Clint Gallagher, you're not getting rid of me as easily as you think." She spoke slowly and distinctly, so there would be no doubt in his mind that she meant exactly what she said. "I have to go back to Seattle for a while—because I promised, and other people are depending on me—but as soon as I finish that project I'll be back—for good. And then you'd better watch out, because I've loved you for as long as I can remember and I know you love me too, and I don't intend to give you up without a fight!'' She paused to take a breath. ''Now—what have you got to say to that?''

''I say it isn't fair to take advantage of a man when he's in a weakened condition.'' Clint didn't sound as if he objected too strenuously, however.

''Okay, the lady loves you, and—if that bull didn't completely knock your brains out—you must love her too,'' the redhaired technician put in, still holding the neck brace. ''So now that that's settled, why don't you kiss her and then let us get on with our work? We've got a job to do, you know.''

''Okay, okay. Just give me a minute.'' Wincing, he pushed himself up to a sitting position, ignoring the technician's alarmed look. ''I want to do this properly.''

''Folks,'' the announcer's voice came over the speaker, ''we may be witnessing romance in the making. Looks like he's sitting up—He's kissing her! And very thoroughly, I'd say.''

A burst of applause rose from the spectators, accompanied by calls of, ''Atta boy, Clint!'' and, '' 'Bout time!''

Shannon twisted out of Clint's arms, a flush staining her cheeks, as the cheering brought her back to rational thought. ''From where I sit, I'd say he's making a remarkable recovery,'' she heard the announcer say with a satisfied chuckle.

She tried to move out of the way to make room for the technicians to get to Clint, but he caught her by the wrist. His grip was surprisingly strong for one who had so recently sustained an injury. He refused to relinquish his hold as the two earnest young men finished treating him and lifted him onto a stretcher, with the assistance of two of the arena men.

She leaned down and gave him one last kiss, to the accompaniment of more cheers from the spectators, just before he was loaded into the ambulance.

Chapter Fourteen

It was almost dark by the time Clint pulled the Jeep into the yard. He'd been out most of the day, clearing brush away from fencelines and cleaning out water holes. In spite of his weariness, he headed for the barn when he alighted from the Jeep, the big ranch dog, Buck, trailing after him companionably. He ought to be able to find something to do in the barn to keep him busy for a while longer.

He reminded himself that he didn't *have* to drive himself until he was so tired that every muscle ached. The jobs he'd been doing weren't so urgent they had to be finished in one day.

Even Len had commented, in his slow, thoughtful way, "Boss, there ain't nothing around here worth killin' yourself over."

Staying occupied was preferable to spending another lonely evening with nothing but his thoughts for company, though. Bethany had been invited on a weeklong camping trip with Melissa's family, and Thelma had taken advantage of the little girl's absence to visit her sister in Billings. With everyone away, his house seemed awfully big and empty.

For a brief period, after Shannon went away, he'd

178

allowed himself to envision her in his home. He could picture her across from him at the kitchen table, next to him on the sofa as they spent their evenings together in companionable silence. . . .

But then the old doubts began to creep in. When Shannon was kneeling beside him in the dust of the rodeo arena, telling him how much she loved him, it was easy to believe she'd really return to him. It wasn't so easy, though, when she was several states away and he hadn't seen her in three weeks.

Oh, he didn't doubt that when she left she had every intention of coming back. But what if the lure of the city, and all that went with it—the lights and glitter, the shows, the fancy restaurants, not to mention a good position with a prestigious company—proved irresistible? Was she really ready to give up all that to bury herself out here in the country?

He realized he was torturing himself needlessly. Just because Valerie had preferred city life to settling down on a ranch with him, there was no reason to think Shannon felt the same.

He'd had several telephone conversations with her since she'd been gone, and each time he'd hung up feeling vaguely disappointed. Talking to her over the phone was a poor substitute for being with her. He wanted to hold her close to him, to feel her lips, warm and yielding, under his. . . .

He drew a heartfelt sigh. "I sure do miss her," he said to Buck, mostly because he was desperate for the sound of a voice—even his own. As if in sympathy, the big golden dog whimpered low in his throat.

The last time Clint had spoken to Shannon—he'd called her at her office one evening when he'd felt as if he'd go crazy if he didn't talk to her—she'd seemed distracted, as if her attention was somewhere else. He tried to tell himself it was just because she was so involved in that project she'd gone back to finish. Maybe he'd interrupted her just as she was at a crucial point. True, she'd given him her work number, and told him to call her there anytime, but he realized it hadn't been such a good idea. It only reminded him that she had another life, one that he wasn't a part of.

And what if it wasn't something that was distracting her, but *someone?* The thought popped, unbidden, into his mind. He tried to push it away but it persisted in nagging at him, like a dog worrying a bone. He had no doubt that boss of hers was interested in more than an employer-employee relationship. And with Shannon putting in such long hours to finish that project, he'd have plenty of opportunity to press his case. They'd be staying at the office late, after everyone else had gone home . . .

Against his will, certain images began to play across Clint's mind. He could picture Shannon sitting at her desk, this Foster guy leaning close to her to view some figures on a computer screen—and getting a little *too* close. Or maybe suggesting they take a break and go out for a bite to eat, then taking her to some intimate little café . . .

He shook his head as if to clear it of the disturbing images. Shannon had told him she loved him, and he had no reason to doubt her.

In spite of his good intentions, though, he couldn't shut out the awareness that if she did change her mind and decide to stay in Seattle, he had nobody to blame but himself. What had he ever done to make her feel he really wanted her to come back to him? Had he ever told her how much she meant to him, that he couldn't live without her?

No, he'd been stubborn and hardheaded and mistrustful. He would have let her go away without anything being settled between them if she hadn't finally taken matters into her own hands and declared that she didn't intend to give him up without a fight.

Absentmindedly, he reached down to pat Buck. "If I had a second chance, I'd make sure she knows how much I love her," he muttered under his breath. Buck's ears perked up and his large, intelligent eyes searched his master's face.

"Maybe it's already too late," Clint went on, as if Buck could understand what he was saying. Shannon was in Seattle this minute, working late with a guy who had made it quite clear he had more in mind than just a business relationship . . .

Are you going to just stand there and do nothing? a little voice in the back of his consciousness asked.

He tried to shrug it off. What *could* he do about it?

Seattle isn't on the other side of the world, that same voice said. *You could catch an early-morning flight and be there in time to have breakfast with her.*

He told himself not to be ridiculous. He had responsibilities, a ranch to run. Tomorrow he was planning to move part of the herd to the summer pasture. And there were repairs to be made on the sprinkler system in the hayfield. He couldn't go flying off on the spur of the moment like some kind of playboy.

Why not?

The words were so clear he almost glanced around to see if someone had spoken aloud. All at once he began to realize that the idea wasn't as outlandish as he'd thought. Len and the rest of the hands could run the ranch without him for a while, and Bethany wouldn't be back until the end of the week.

"What do you think about it, Buck?" he asked. "Should I go to Seattle and tell Shannon I love her?"

Buck tilted his head, as if considering this. Wagging his tail, he emitted a short, sharp bark.

"You think I should go for it, huh?" Clint said. "You know, that's exactly what *I* think."

With an air of determination, he turned and headed for the house. A few minutes later he had the phone directory out and was looking up *Airlines* in the Yellow Pages.

Maggie, the receptionist at Software Specialties, looked up from her desk. "May I help y—"

Her voice failed her as her gaze slowly took in the tall man standing in front of her. All six feet—and then some—of him. And every inch of him, from his thick hair down to his ornately tooled boots, was drop-dead gorgeous!

Boots? She leaned forward slightly to peer over her desk for a closer look. Yes, he *was* wearing boots. But even if he hadn't been, he definitely didn't look "Seattle." Although his attire was properly business-like, there was something about the cut of his well-fitting suit that gave it a vaguely western look. He seemed decidedly out of place in this sedate office. He exuded an air of power and vitality, as if he ought to be out taming a wild bronc, or—or wrestling a steer or something.

His presence seemed to fill the small outer office.

The effect was quite overwhelming. Although Maggie was close to fifty and had been happily married for twenty-five years, she could feel her cheeks growing warm. Men like this didn't turn up at Software Specialties every day. Telling her suddenly erratic pulse to behave, Maggie tried again. "May I help you?"

"Yes, ma'am. I'd like to see Shannon McCrae."

His drawl was warm and rich, like honey. Maggie found she was having a little trouble catching her breath.

"Is she in?"

"What?" Maggie asked vaguely.

"Shannon McCrae. Is she in?"

With an effort, Maggie pulled herself together. "Yes, she's in her office." Automatically, her hand went to the intercom. Then she thought better of it. She needed to put some distance between herself and this altogether too attractive cowboy. "I'll—ah—just tell her you're here."

As she beat a hasty retreat down the corridor toward Shannon's office, it occurred to Maggie that she hadn't gotten his name. *No matter,* she thought. She wasn't going back out there and embarrass herself further. Besides, when a man was as attractive as he was, who cared about names?

She was aware that Shannon was planning to leave the company to return to some little town in Montana or Wyoming, or somewhere out there in the wilderness. Privately, Maggie had thought she had to be crazy to give up a promising career to bury herself out in the middle of nowhere. But if that guy in the waiting room was the reason she was going back, she'd have to be crazy *not* to.

As Shannon studied her computer screen she rubbed her fingers across her forehead, as if she could massage away the tiredness. She'd been coming in early and staying late in an effort to get this job finished as soon as possible. If all went well she should be done in another day or two. Then she'd be on her way back to Liberty—and to Clint.

Paul had been disappointed when she told him she was only here temporarily, but he'd also been understanding. "I wish I could persuade you to stay," he'd said, "but I have the feeling there's something more than homesickness that's calling you back to Montana." Then he'd put his hands on her shoulders and kissed her very gently on the forehead. "I wish you all the happiness you deserve."

She hoped she was doing the right thing by going back. The thought kept popping into her mind—despite her best efforts to shut it out—that maybe she *should* have waited for Clint to tell her he wanted her to come back instead of forcing the issue. Although he'd been joking when he said it wasn't fair to take advantage of a man when he was in a weakened condition, there was a grain of truth in his words.

But it had been almost time for her to leave for the airport, and when she'd seen him lying there on the ground injured she'd realized she couldn't go away without telling him how much she loved him . . .

Her thoughts were interrupted as her door flew open and Maggie slipped inside her office as if she were being chased. "Maggie, what is it?" Shannon asked, noting that the normally self-composed receptionist seemed slightly agitated.

"There's a . . . a gentleman to see you."

Shannon waited. When Maggie didn't offer any more information, she prompted, "A gentleman?"

"I, ah, didn't get his name."

That was odd, Shannon thought. Maggie was usually a model of efficiency. She took her duties seriously, and *nobody* got past her eagle eye without giving a name and a reason for requesting entrance into the inner realms of Software Specialties.

"Could you be a pal and put him off?" Shannon asked. "I'm almost finished here, and I—"

"I think you'll want to see this guy."

Shannon gave her a curious look. "Why? If he's a prospective client there won't be much point in my seeing him. I'll be out of here in another day or two, you know. He'd be better off talking to Paul."

"Maybe you ought to tell him that yourself—"

At that moment, Clint's tall form appeared in the doorway. "The door was open," he explained, "so I just, ah . . ." The rest of his words seemed to be forgotten as his eyes met Shannon's.

At first Shannon was certain she was imagining things. She was tired—and she'd thought about Clint so much that her mind was playing tricks on her.

But he was definitely real—so real that she longed to lean her head against his broad chest and rest in his strong, warm embrace. She restrained herself, though, as it occurred to her that if he was here—in Seattle— it must be because something was wrong. Maybe he'd come to tell her he thought it might be better if they didn't continue their relationship.

She came around her desk as if she were sleepwalking. "Wh-what are you doing here?" she got out, steeling her emotions for his reply.

"I went to your apartment, but you'd already left for work, so I came here."

"No, I mean, in Seattle—"

"I had to talk to you. After you left I realized I'd never told you how much I love you. I-I was afraid if you didn't know, you might change your mind about coming back to me."

As his words sank in, a bubble of happiness burst inside her and spread through her entire being. "And you came all the way to Seattle to tell me?" She found it hard to speak around the lump in her throat.

"If you didn't come back—well, my life wouldn't be worth much without you," he replied simply, as if that said it all.

A watery fullness welled up in Shannon's eyes. "Oh, Clint . . ."

During this exchange Maggie had been looking from Shannon to Clint and back again. Now she decided it was time these two had some privacy.

Neither of them noticed as she stepped into the corridor. Taking one last peek before she softly closed the door, she saw that the space between Shannon and Clint had somehow closed, and she was in his arms.

A little smile played around her mouth as Maggie made her way back to her desk. She did love a happy ending.